An Augath

ANNIE SEATON

Augathella Short and Sweet: 5

AUGATHELLA SHORT AND SWEETS

An Augathella Surprise

An Augathella Baby

An Augathella Spring

An Augathella Christmas

An Augathella Wedding

An Augathella Easter

An Augathella Ball

Following on from:

THE AUGATHELLA GIRLS

Book 1: Outback Roads –The Nanny

Book 2: Outback Sky – The Pilot

Book 3: Outback Escape – The Sister

Book 4: Outback Winds – The Jillaroo

Book 5: Outback Dawn – The Visitor

Book 6: Outback Moonlight – The Rogue

Book 7: Outback Dust – The Drifter

Book 8: Outback Hope – The Farmer

CHAPTER 1

Rosie
March

'Are we crazy moving so far away to a place we've never even been to?' Rosie Renouf reached over and placed her hand on her husband's knee as he changed back a gear in the truck.

'There's not one bit of crazy between us. Just great choices.' Lex shook his head. 'And a lot of luck.'

'I don't call it luck, sweetie. It was all Chloe. And I totally trust her.'

'I do too, and I guess I have to accept that, but my logical brain says it was luck. It actually scares me a bit.'

'What does?

'How she is. What she knows.'

'Chloe has a gift.'

'She sure does. Anyway, we're only about

ten kilometres from Augathella so get ready to see your new home.'

A quiver of anticipation ran through Rosie and she tried to stay calm. They were almost there; three months of planning, purchasing, and organising and Lex was about to get his farm.

And they were getting a new start in life. If anyone had told her that they would be moving to the Aussie outback within two years of emigrating from London, she would have said they were crazy. But they hadn't met Chloe and Greg then.

Now they were the crazy ones.

The highway from Charleville to Augathella had a couple of slight hills, but the road had been fairly flat most of the way since they'd left Brisbane three days ago. Lex had enjoyed driving the big truck and had even suggested that he might take up truck driving—with a grin and a glance at Rosie—as a new career. She didn't take the bait. Her husband knew what he wanted to do here in Augathella. They all did, and there were exciting times ahead.

Rosie enjoyed looking around; the landscape was so different from what she had expected. She must admit she'd had her doubts when they'd chosen this town because she envisioned it being in the middle of the red, dusty outback.

However, here, along the edges of the highway just south of their destination, thick, silver and pale green trees filled the paddocks. Some of the trees reminded her of the forest near her childhood home in England.

When Rosie called her mum and dad to tell them that they were moving from Brisbane to the outback, her mother was horrified. 'Oh dear, darling, I don't know that we'll ever be able to come and visit you there now. I don't think I could cope with the heat. You'll have to come home and see us every year.'

Her mum's request to visit would have been impossible up until recently—airfares had been out of reach— and even though they could now afford to go back to the UK for visits, Rosie hoped her parents would come and visit. She knew they'd love it here.

Even in the outback.

Her parents were stuck in their ways, and she vowed to never let herself get like that.

She kept her voice even. 'That's why air-conditioners were invented, Mum, and we will have one in every room. We're going to build our beautiful family home out there on a small property. I'd so love you and Dad to come and visit. We'll book your tickets for you.'

There was a long silence, then, 'You know your dad won't fly.'

'I'll book you on a cruise ship.'

'He can't swim either.'

Rosie's eyes swam with tears and she gave

up. 'Okay. We'll come home for a visit once we get settled.'

'I still can't understand what's happened to you,' her mum said. 'First, you leave home and move to London. Next thing I know you're heading off to another country with Lex. And now he's dragging you out to the dangerous outback. It's about time you settled down and had children instead of going off on mad adventures. You read way too much Enid Blyton when you were a child.'

Rosie had stifled a giggle at that, but she knew if she told her parents what had caused this "adventure" they would have been even more shocked. She shook her head as she thought back to that fateful night in December. She and Lex still had to pinch themselves to believe it wasn't a dream.

Their adventure had all started when her best friend, Chloe, told them what she wanted to do. She and Chloe had met in the local supermarket the week after Lex and Rosie had arrived in Australia to start their new lives. Rosie had a casual job there. They had struck up a conversation and had quickly become firm friends. Lex and Chloe's husband, Greg, had hit it off too, and soon their friendship group expanded. They had more friends in Australia than they had ever made in London.

Chloe's suggestion was delivered at a barbeque at Rob and Suzanne's place in early December; it had certainly got a response.

'What?' their friend, Leah, had exclaimed. 'You're crazy, Chloe!' Leah, a teacher, was a very sensible, straight-down-the-line sort of friend.

'Crazy?' Chloe shook her head. 'No, I'm not. I know this. All we need is fifty dollars from each of us. One hundred per couple. So, we'll have five hundred dollars to invest.'

Leah shook her head again. 'Are you sure it will have a return?'

Chloe's smile was sweet and gentle. 'It's okay, Leah. If you don't want to be a part of it, that's fine. When you commit, I'll tell you.'

Mick, Leah's husband lifted his beer glass and chuckled. 'We're in, babe. Nothing ventured, nothing gained.'

Leah rolled her eyes at Mick. 'Okay. I guess we're in.'

'We are, aren't we, Lex?' Rosie had gone along with Chloe, even though she was as sceptical as Lex and the rest of the group.

'Yep, we'll be here with bells on,' Lex agreed. 'In for a penny, in for a pound.'

Mick scratched his head and grinned at Lex. 'You're such a pommy, mate. Half the time I don't understand what you're saying. Pennies and bells?'

Lex grinned back at him.

'If you're not willing to risk the unusual, you have to settle for the ordinary.' Rob held up his beer. 'We're in.'

'Us too,' Peter said, but Gemma frowned; Rose knew Peter and Gemma did it tough with a big mortgage.

'Okay, no pain, no gain.' Chloe's husband Greg smiled. 'And if I say no to my lovely wife and if what she says is going to happen, does happen, I'll be in the doghouse for the rest of my life.

'If?' Chloe said, her delicate eyebrows raised.

'*When* it happens,' Greg corrected.

'But what's going to happen?' Suzanne asked. Everyone waited for Chloe to answer.

'Change,' was her enigmatic reply.

Rosie and Lex, Chloe and Greg, Leah and Mick, Rob and Suzanne, and newer to their group, Peter and Gemma, had become a very tight friendship group even though they were all very different personalities. Some of them were dissatisfied with their public service careers. Life during COVID-19 had made them rethink their work and home priorities.

'A change would be nice,' Gemma said, 'but Chloe, we have to eat, and we've got a mortgage to pay. One day I'd love to own a hairdressing salon.'

Rosie nodded. 'I know, and we've talked about this over the last couple of years. Lex would love to have a farm like he grew up on at home.'

'This is home now, love,' Lex corrected.

'It is. But some of us are trapped in jobs we don't enjoy anymore. True?'

Everyone nodded slowly, except for Rob and Suzanne.

'We're content,' Suzanne said. 'Aren't we, Rob?'

Rob nodded. 'Pretty happy with our lot, but we'll throw in a hundred bucks. What are we investing in?'

Rosie couldn't help looking around the deck of their luxury apartment. Of the five couples, Rob and Suzanne had the highest income, and they were the only ones with children. Whenever they socialised, their kids were sent off to babysitters.

'Change. We're investing in change.' Chloe said. 'Trust me.'

Rosie and Lex exchanged glances. Chloe was always impulsive and positive.

But she was always right. If she said there was going to be a change, they needed to listen to what she was saying because it was likely to happen.

'On the Thursday before Christmas you're all coming to our place for dinner,' she said.

'Should be right with us; I'll have to check

my roster,' Mick, who was in the water police, nodded. 'I could be on night work that week.'

'Why not the weekend, Chloe?' Lex asked.

Chloe stood. She spread her arms wide as though embracing them all. 'Because that's the night we're going to win Powerball,' she said.

Rosie smiled as she noted the variety of pulled faces and eye-rolls. 'Sounds good to me,' she said, not wanting to put a dampener on Chloe's enthusiasm, despite quietly believing that this time her best friend was wrong.

Chloe had had the toughest time of all of them recently. Not financially, but emotionally. When she was working at home during the COVID-19 lockdown, she and Greg had decided to start a family.

'I can stay at home and work, and look after the baby,' she'd said excitedly.

Now with Chloe just coming out of another failed round of IVF, Rosie knew Greg would do anything to make Chloe happy. He might be as sceptical as the rest of them, but he adored Chloe.

'I'll buy the champagne,' he said, putting his arm around Chloe's shoulder. 'Dan Murphy's got a sale on this week.'

##

Two weeks later, they were crammed on the small deck at the back of Chloe and Greg's rented house enjoying a pre-Christmas barbeque. It was a very different venue to Rob and Suzanne's deck overlooking the Brisbane River.

'Okay, you lot.' Chloe stood and pointed to the door. 'Come into the living room, it's ten minutes until the draw.' She turned to Greg. 'Is the champagne cold, sweetheart?'

'Sure, is, love.'

Rosie's heart went out to Chloe. She was pretty sure the rest of the group had forgotten they were here for the draw. It hadn't been brought up in conversation yet.

But as they waited in front of the television, dreams were thrown around, and the conversation turned to their futures and what they would do if they won.

Chloe sat there quietly, her face alight with her ever-present sweet smile.

'We're certainly not going to go back to the UK, no matter what your mum says,' Lex said with a glance at Rosie. 'We'd probably move to somewhere out west where we can have a bit of land.'

Greg nodded. 'We'd be in that. I'd start my own business in a small town somewhere.'

Gemma turned to her husband. 'We'd move too. We just can't afford to live in the city anymore. We've been talking about moving for a while now. And we've made the move, haven't we, love?'

Peter looked embarrassed. 'I feel like a failure, but I can't stand going into the bank every day and trying to sell products to customers who can't afford it. I've put my notice in and we're moving. We've got enough savings to last us three months or so.'

Gemma reached out and touched Peter's hand. 'I'm leaving the salon and we're going down the coast after Christmas to visit my sister, and then we're going to decide where we'll move to.'

Chloe's smile widened as she switched the large flatscreen television on. 'Listen guys, after tonight, you won't need to worry. I was thinking about a tropical island or some land we could all buy together. What do you think of that?'

Mick nodded. 'That would be a dream come true for me.'

'And me,' Lex said.

The conversations continued and the dreams became more farfetched as the ads flickered across the screen in front of them. On the dot of eight-thirty, Chloe turned the volume up. 'Okay everyone, shush, pay attention. We have to get the right vibe going. I've written our numbers on the whiteboard in the order they'll come out. Greg, turn it around please.'

Rosie bit her lip as Greg walked across the room and picked up the small whiteboard lying face down on the coffee table. Poor Chloe; she knew how disappointed her friend was going to be. With any luck, they might win twenty dollars and that wouldn't go far, split five ways.

As the blue and white balls tumbled in the two transparent spheres, they waited. The blue balls dropped from the left one at a time and a tense and disbelieving stillness took hold of the five couples who were now glued to the screen.

By the time the sixth number had dropped,

the room was silent. Everyone's eyes were wide. Rosie grabbed Lex's hand and held it tightly. Chloe sat back on the lounge with a smile on her face. Not one word was said. The seventh blue ball dropped out, and there was a huge intake of breath.

'Oh my God, oh my God.' Leah's voice was shaking. 'We've got seven numbers.'

'And now we'll get the Powerball because that's the number I chose,' Chloe said. 'I threw dice for the others and as you can see the universe was looking after me.'

Rosie looked at the board which only held seven numbers. 'What number did you choose for the Powerball, Chloe?' she asked breathlessly. The air could've been cut with a knife as they waited for Chloe to answer and watched the white balls tumble and roll, and then one white ball rose to the top

'Number six,' Chloe replied confidently.

They all leaned forward as the white ball reached the top.

'Is it a six or a nine?' Greg said as he dropped to the sofa beside Chloe and clutched her hand. Stunned disbelief held them in thrall as the white ball, number six, dropped to join the others and the number flashed on the screen.

Chloe sat back and held up the printed ticket. 'Now who'll doubt me next time?'

Rosie found it hard to breathe, and she wondered if she was having an asthma attack. Lex nudged her shoulder and she let go of the breath she'd been holding.

Lex's arms went around Rosie as she swept her gaze around their friends. 'Am I dreaming or did we just get six numbers and the Powerball?'

'We did,' said Chloe. 'One hundred million dollars.'

CHAPTER 2

Rosie

The planning- January

'A cattle property,' Lex said, as the guys sat around the fire pit at Chloe and Greg's new apartment; Chloe had insisted that they temporarily move somewhere nice while they made their plans. Rosie smiled at her husband as she brought out the first two bowls of salad and put them on the table.

'A cattle property with a beautiful homestead,' she agreed.

'Nope.' Mick shook his head. 'It's going to be a fishing boat for me.'

'For *us*,' Leah chimed in. 'I get to choose too. I've been looking at brochures.'

'I thought being on the water for work would make you want to escape inland,' Greg chimed in.

Mick shook his head again. 'I love being on the water. It's the only good thing about my job.'

'I think we're making our decisions the best way. Slow and considered,' Rosie said. Once the euphoria of that night had worn off, they had all agreed not to tell anyone about their amazing win; the five couples hadn't even shared the news with any of their families, although a couple of the looks Rosie had seen between Rob and Suzanne had made her wonder.

When they'd messaged the group to say that they were happy to take their fifth share and remain independent of any plans, Rosie hadn't been surprised.

The discussions between the other four couples over the past weeks had been intense, full of fantasy and farfetched dreams, and the occasional disagreement as the suggestions became more ridiculous. As always, Chloe was the voice of reason. Four weeks after the amazing windfall, she messaged their group chat and called them all together for tonight's barbeque.

'What would we do without you, Chloe?' Rosie hugged her best friend when they arrived.

'You would have all quit your jobs by now.'

'We've gone close,' Rosie said.

Their lifestyles hadn't changed since that earth-shattering moment when the Lotteries office had confirmed their win an hour after they had watched the draw. Rosie and Lex were still living in the same rented accommodation, driving the same vehicles, and under Chloe's sage advice, they were taking a considered approach to what they were going to do.

Sailing boats, overseas trips, huge homes

with swimming pools on acreage; all had been discussed. This was the first time Lex had spoken of the dream that Rosie knew he had always held. Before the win, they'd discussed going out west to escape the city and live a slower lifestyle.

'Right,' Chloe said as they all sat down to eat when the barbequed meat was on the table.

'I still can't believe we're barbequing Wagyu steak,' Lex said as he passed the meat tray across the table.

'A bit different to rissoles, but I do still prefer sausages,' Rosie said with a cheeky grin.

'Well, now that we can afford the best, you can buy gourmet sausages,' Chloe said.

Rosie chuckled. 'Nothing wrong with Woollies bangers. It's what I'm used to.'

When they finished eating, Chloe stood and tapped a spoon on the side of her wine glass.

'Rightio, guys. Tonight's the night,' she

said. 'Tonight, we're going to decide if we're going to go our separate ways, like Rob and Suzanne to follow our dreams. Or will we do it together? Our tropical islands, our fancy houses, and our fancy speedboats.' Chloe paused and looked at each of them as they sat around the table, their attention riveted on her. 'Or are we going to do something that makes a difference to other people?'

'You are the most beautiful person, Chloe. You really ground us all, you know.' Rosie smiled as they all looked at Chloe. 'If it wasn't for you, we wouldn't be having this conversation.'

'Well, I figure as none of us have got money worries for the rest of our lives, we *can* follow our hearts. But all the things we've talked about, the things we can buy now, do we need them? Do we need flash boats and fancy cars? Will those possessions make us happy?'

Lex and Rosie looked at each other. They each knew in their hearts what would make Chloe and Greg happy but all the money in the world wouldn't bring that to them.

'What does your heart want? I want you all to just think about it quietly for ten minutes. Close your eyes and let your heart tell you. Feel what you want deep in your heart, what will make you happy.' Her voice trembled a little and Rosie's heart broke for her friend. She and Lex weren't ready to start a family yet, but Chloe and Greg had been keen from the minute they married. But they had faced disappointment after disappointment in the three IVF attempts, and Rosie knew that it had been expensive.

'Rosie,' Chloe said, 'I can hear your mind ticking over from here. I know what you're focusing on. Close down your thoughts and go with your heart. What *you* want, not me.'

Rosie closed her eyes and smiled as Lex reached for her hand. They were on the same wavelength. Lex had been teaching, and she had been casual nursing, working long hours, and they both came home the same night and announced to each other they were leaving their jobs once they'd decided what to do with their share.

Greg worked at an accountant's office at Wynnum. Chloe had part-time paralegal work in the city but didn't find it fulfilling. The police force, health, law, and education; it hadn't been a coincidence how several of them had already decided to change careers before the win.

All except Rob and Suzanne; they were content with their lot—Suzanne didn't work, and Rob owned a real estate agency. They hadn't said much since the win.

Rosie had wondered if the restlessness

about their various careers had been some sort of premonition Chloe had channelled. Maybe deep down they'd known this was going to happen, without recognising and acknowledging what it was.

Whoops, Rosie realised that she was thinking too much. She closed her eyes tightly and let her heart take over. The time went in a flash, and Chloe put her hands on her knees and looked around the group.

'Right, everyone, it's time. Rosie, you're first. What does your heart tell you? One sentence.'

'Moving from the city, living in a small town, doing something that makes me happy and helps other people. I don't know what, but it will happen.'

'Lex?'

'Being with Rosie in her small town, and having our farm.'

'Mick?'

'Um, staying in the police force. Making a difference but not in the city, and with a boat for the holidays.'

'Leah?' Chloe prompted.

Leah smiled at her husband. 'I'll follow Mick to his small town, and go back to teaching. Move into special education if I can, that's what I love to do.'

'Pete?' Chloe said.

'I'd like to start a department store in a small country town. I remember growing up in Longreach and what an eye-opener it was the times we went to Brisbane. All the shops were like Aladdin's Cave to me. I want to take that to country kids and their parents.' He glanced at Gemma. 'And of course, with a hairdressing salon and a café in the store. Sorry, Chloe, that was more than a sentence.'

'This is all sounding fabulous.' Chloe

looked at Greg. 'Sweetheart, do you want to describe our dream?'

'You go, love,' Greg said smiling at his wife. 'After all, our life changes are due to you.'

'A toast to Chloe,' Peter said, lifting his glass and everyone lifted theirs as well. 'Thank you, Chloe.'

Chloe's cheeks were pink as she stood and lifted her hands, and then brought her thumbs and index fingers together at the tips, extending the rest of her fingers. She'd told Rosie a few weeks ago the hand gesture was called the *Gyan Mudra* and its purpose was to increase knowledge and wisdom.

She was a wise, gentle soul, that was for sure. Her dark brown eyes were expressive; Lex had commented when he met her that Chloe's eyes were the window to her soul. Her eyes always expressed her calm and gentle nature. Even when her IVF hadn't been successful, she had seen the positive side to it.

'Thank you,' she said. 'Okay, now, the big question is, with all our dreams, do we all move together or do we go our separate ways? Don't even think about it. What does your heart tell you?'

Rosie looked around at her friends, all nodding. 'Together?' she said tentatively. 'It would be nice to move to a new town and all start our new directions together.'

A chorus of, 'Together, for sure,' answered her question.

'Okay, let's get the map out.' Chloe's voice was brisk now.

Rosie expected her to pull out her phone, but Chloe walked to the buffet along the wall and retrieved an old-fashioned paper map of Queensland.

'Boy, that's an old one,' Greg said. 'Where did you get that from?'

'It was Mum and Dad's. We used to travel around a lot when I was a kid. I found it in their stuff when I cleaned out the house last year. Something told me it would come in handy one day, and it has.' She spread the map in the middle of the table and smoothed the edges down where they were threatening to curl. 'Okay, stand up and then close your eyes. I want everybody to lean forward and put their finger on the map.'

CHAPTER 3

March - Laura

'Aunty Laura, look at that truck.' Petie tugged Laura's hand as they stood on the footpath outside Meat Ant Park.

'Wow, it's a beauty,' she said, smiling to herself. Spending time with her three nephews had resulted in her picking up several new Aussie phrases.

A large truck drove slowly down the street. Obviously a furniture removalist, the truck had a bright swirly logo on it. One of the prettiest designs Laura had ever seen: swirls of rainbow with the company logo in huge purple letters: **A New Life.**

She wondered idly if it was some religious group travelling through the outback, but the truck pulled up about a hundred metres down from the park where two huge sheds had been built over the past six weeks. There had been much speculation in town as to what was going on there.

At the same time, a dozen or so houses on the edge of town had been demolished, and building work had commenced. No one seemed to know who was responsible. The builders had come out from Brisbane, and the new dwellings were going up at the rate of knots.

'It's the biggest truck I've ever seen,' Petie said. 'I wonder if Dad would do that with the cattle truck.'

'Draw pretty pictures on it?' Laura chuckled. 'I can't see your dad having a purple rainbow cattle truck.'

'I'm going to ask him,' Petie said, a serious frown wrinkling his little forehead. 'When he gets home.'

Laura held out her hand for Petie to take as they crossed the road. Her brother-in-law,

Braden, was away at a cattlemen's conference in Longreach, and Callie was working extra days at the school this week because Kimberley Riordan had been off sick; Callie was taking over her classes.

It wasn't common knowledge yet that Kimberley's upset stomach was morning sickness. As the hospital midwife, Laura had talked Kimberley through the best ways to deal with it a couple of weeks ago, but Kimberley was considering leaving school early as nothing was working; she had morning sickness all day.

Laura knew if that happened Callie would be working more days. Harry was away for two days too, and Laura had a few days off from the hospital, so she'd volunteered to look after her youngest nephew. He had a bit of a tummy upset, and Callie had been going to stay home with him. Laura had called her by chance that morning and had been happy to offer to mind

Petie. Since she'd moved to Augathella, the time she'd spent with the three boys had been precious.

She shook her head, thinking back to the Laura that she had been in those days—so unhappy and bitter—and how much her life had changed. Since she'd arrived in this small outback town and met Braden, her brother-in-law, again, and his new wife and her three delightful nephews, and fallen in love with Dr Harry, life had been wonderful. Assisting in the delivery of Braden and Callie's twins had been a privilege. Laura's only regret was that she hadn't come over before the accident that had taken her sister's life.

As always when she thought of Julia, her eyes welled with tears. Julia would be so proud of her boys and Braden, the success that he was making of their property. But equally, if she knew Braden's new wife, Laura knew that Julia would have been happy to see what a beautiful woman Braden had chosen to marry and become a mother to her three boys.

Even though life was good, a tiny glimmer of worry tugged at Laura as they walked along.

Harry had been distant for the last couple of weeks, and she wondered if there was something wrong. Had he decided he didn't want to be with her anymore? No, it couldn't be that; she knew that he loved her. Was he unwell? Was he getting restless? Did he want to move away? Now that Laura had found her family, she was quite content living in Augathella. She loved her job as a midwife at the hospital, she adored Harry, and she was very content. She didn't want to go anywhere else, but if she had to make the choice, she knew what she would do. Harry was the most important person in her life, and she'd follow.

She loved him. It was as simple as that.

Harry had lost his first wife to illness and he often looked at her with a look of wonder in his eyes.

'I don't know why you picked an old guy like me,' he once said.

'Old? You're only seven years older than me, so if that's old, that makes me old too!'

Harry had smiled his gentle smile. The one that always sent that shiver of longing shooting through Laura. 'But I can see how much you love those boys, and I know you'd love to have children.'

'Harry, I love you, and I'm happy with you, and that's all I want. Besides I'm almost forty. I've left my run too late. I'm happy being an aunty.'

But she did worry that he was thinking of leaving her to give her the chance to be a mother.

Petie tugged at her hand. 'Let's walk down

and see where the truck's going and what comes out of it.' He looked at up her, his expression innocent. 'Then maybe we could have an ice cream over at the coffee shop. My tummy's good now. What do you think about that, Aunty Laura?'

Laura smiled, knowing that she'd give in. 'Hmm. I'll have to think about that.'

They walked along the footpath and stopped outside the first shed. It was built out of timber and had a red tin roof. A double set of glass doors was set in the middle of the front with a small, covered porch, but the doors were papered up so you couldn't see inside.

'Look, Aunty Laura, what do you think it's going to be? A shop? Is it a toy shop, do you think? There's a sign ready to go up. What does it say?'

Laura shook her head. 'It says: **What You Want, What You Need – Come and See Us:**

A New Life Store.'

'I need a new bike,' Petie said hopefully.

Laura frowned. It sounded like a church to her. 'Come on. We'll go to the coffee shop.'

As they reached the footpath outside the second shed, the passenger door of the truck opened and a pretty young woman with long blonde hair climbed out. Her smile was wide as she looked at Laura.

'Good morning,' she said. 'Isn't it a lovely day!'

'Good morning,' Laura replied.

'I love your truck! Can I have a ride in it one day?' Petie dropped Laura's hand and pointed at the truck.

The young woman smiled. 'If your mum says yes, I'm sure you could.'

'That's not my mum; that's my Aunty Laura. My mum is at the school; she's a teacher, and I was sick.'

'I hope you're better now.'

'I'm okay. I just had a pain in the belly because I ate too many apricots last night.'

'I love apricots too,' the pretty woman said.

'You should've seen when I...'

Laura put a hand over Petie's mouth. 'That's enough, Petie.' He'd already given her a vivid description of what his upset stomach had done through the night, and—thank goodness—with her nursing background, she was able to cope with the graphic description. 'That's private, Petie.' She smiled at the young woman. 'Hello, my name is Laura, and as you already know, this is my nephew. His name is Petie.'

'And I have a dog called Apricot too,' Petie said. 'And two big brothers, and a little brother and sister. I'm in the middle.'

'Hello, Laura, and hello, Petie. I'm Rosie. Rosie Renouf.' She turned and spread her arms wide. 'And this is our new store.'

'You've moved to town?' Laura asked.

'We have. And we're all very happy about it.'

Laura couldn't help asking. 'Are you building one of the new houses in town?'

'No,' Rose replied. 'Our house is being built out of town a little way, but we haven't seen it yet. We've just arrived.' She glanced across at the shed as a tall broad-shouldered man came out of the door at the side. 'This is my husband Lex; Lex, this is Laura and Petie.'

'Hello, lovely to meet you.' He lifted his hand with a casual wave. 'Come on, Rosie; come and have a look. I've unlocked both and they're amazing.'

Laura was itching to have a look but didn't feel it would be the right thing to ask.

'I'll be there in a minute. I'm just getting to know some of the townspeople. Our townspeople,' she said, with a beaming smile.

Lex looked down at his wife with a kind smile before he looked back at Laura. 'We've just arrived and still have to unload the truck and get ourselves settled. We're going to live in the shed until our houses are ready.'

'Houses?' Laura asked.

'Our friends are a little way behind us on the road. That's their houses being built across town. We haven't had a look yet.'

Laura was intrigued but didn't want to seem too curious. 'Well, welcome to town. We sometimes have a weekend picnic in the park near the river when new people arrive in town,' she said. 'It's great to see how many new couples are moving to the district.'

'There's eight of us,' Rosie said.

'We need another picnic. Aunty Laura, can you organise one? Soon?' Petie jumped up and down with excitement. 'With another sausage sizzle and kids' races like the last one when

Mummy had a baby in the toilet, but there were two! Meggie and Munro.'

Rosie crouched down level with Petie. 'Wow, how exciting. I like this town more every minute. A welcome barbecue sounds fabulous.' She turned to her husband. 'Maybe we could have something out the back of the shop; we could have a big opening and invite everyone in town.'

'Rosie, Rosie, slowly, slowly,' her husband said, but his smile was wide.

'Come on, Petie, we'd better shake a leg if you want an ice-cream. School finishes soon.' Laura reached out to take his hand.

'Can I ask one question?' he asked.

Laura nodded. 'Just one.'

Petie leaned closer to Rosie who was still at his eye level. He dropped his voice. 'Do you sell bikes in your shop?'

CHAPTER 4

Jenna

Jenna smiled as Laura and Petie walked up the front steps of her vintage tearoom. She picked up her order pad and hurried over to Emily and Luke to take their order before Laura and Petie settled. It had been a quiet morning. Emily and Luke were firmly ensconced in the corner, deep in discussion.

Ophelia, Emily's daughter was being babysat at Ruth Mason's house and Jenna wondered what they were discussing so seriously. Emily and Luke had planned to marry in January before school resumed, but the sudden closure of the pub for renovations had put paid to their plans for the reception. Braden Cartwright had offered *Kilcoy Station*, but Emily and Luke had decided to wait until the pub was open again.

When the pub had closed without notice, Jenna had quickly offered the tearooms for the reception.

'Thank you, Jenna, but no,' Emily said instantly. 'As much as it would be lovely to have it here where Luke and I met up again, I don't want you to be working at our wedding. And I know you, you wouldn't be able to help yourself.' Her smile was wide. 'Plus, I want you to be my bridesmaid,' Emily had said.

Jenna was touched. 'Oh, I'd love that. If you don't want to have it here or at Braden and Callie's place, I guess the only other place in Augathella *is* the pub.'

She crossed the room and stood beside their table. 'Ready to order, guys?' she asked.

'Just the usual coffees, thanks, Jenna. Nothing to eat,' Emily said. 'Listen, have you heard any more about the pub? Luke heard a whisper over the weekend that it's been sold. Have you heard that?'

'No, I thought it was being renovated. It's all rather sudden and hush-hush though, isn't it?'

'Renovations *have* started already,' Luke said. 'So hopefully it won't take too long.'

'Josh said there's a lot of building happening around town and it all seems to be a bit top-secret too.'

'There is a lot of change in the wind. More people moving here: a new police sergeant, a new nurse at the hospital to replace Bec, and a new teacher at the school too. Callie was telling me last weekend.'

'Where's Bec going? She and Matt aren't leaving town, are they?' Jenna frowned.

'No, apparently Bec's been offered a job working a community role with the council. She was telling me the other day she wants to work with young people for a while.'

'She'll be great doing that. Bec's great fun. She'll be good for our town. So will more new people here,' Jenna said. 'I love living in Augie. It's great to see life being injected into it. Reg would have enjoyed what's going on.' She blinked away a tear. Jenna was still grieving for the grandfather she had known so briefly.

'And there are those two big sheds built up near the park.' Emily's face was animated. 'I'd love to know what's going on there.'

'The town is certainly coming ahead,' Luke said. 'Okay, come on, girls, let's get back to the wedding. I guess we've decided to wait for the pub to re-open?' A frown marred his forehead.

'Do you want to wait, Luke?' Emily reached over and put her hand on his.

'Not really,' he said. 'But I do want to celebrate in Augathella. We've decided to base ourselves here, Jenna. I can manage my work from here. My boss in Narrabri has agreed.'

'That's great news,' Jenna said. 'I'll go and get your coffee.'

'Hang on a minute,' Emily said. 'I've got a better idea.'

'An idea?' Luke asked.

'Jenna, could you take a day off from the tearooms?'

'Yes, Ellie can handle it by herself now.'

Emily reached over and took Luke's hand. 'Why don't we go down to Charleville next week, or as soon as we can book the celebrant, and get married there? Jenna can be our witness. And then we can have the reception in a few weeks when the pub opens up.'

Luke's face lit up. 'I think that's a great idea. How about I call the celebrant now?'

Emily smiled as he pulled his phone out of his shirt pocket and headed out to the front porch.

'Sounds like a plan's in place,' Jenna said. 'Just let me know what day and I'll get Ellie to open up. Are you going to take some time off school to go away?'

Emily shook her head. 'No, we'll wait until the Easter school holidays. We'll take Ophelia down to the Gold Coast.'

Emily's smile was wide as Jenna made her way over to the coffee machine and put the order up. 'No food, just coffee,' Jenna said to Ellie before she made her way over to Laura and Petie who were waiting near the door.

'Hello, you pair. Sit wherever you like and I'll get your order going.'

'I've got a huge favour to ask,' Laura said. 'The coffee shop in town is closed, the pub's not open and we can't get ice cream for Petie anywhere. Although I am wondering whether he should have it or not; he's off school with an upset stomach, but Petie's insisting it's all right now.'

'I got rid of the food that made me sick. Jenna you should have seen—'

'Enough, Petie.' Laura shook her head.

'Oops, sorry, Aunty Laura.' His eyes were wide and innocent. 'But I really need ice cream to make me completely better.'

Jenna hid her smile as she held the order pad. 'Well, you're in luck, Petie. I have ice cream and I have lots of toppings: caramel, strawberry, lime, and passionfruit. As long as your aunty says it's okay.'

Laura nodded.

'I'll have all of them, please,' Petie said. 'Mixed up swirly on a double scoop of ice cream.'

'Obviously feeling better then. What about you, Laura?'

'I'll have a skinny cap please, Jenna.'

'Cake?' Jenna asked.

'Tempt me. I'm starving.' Laura's smile made her even prettier. 'What have you got today?'

'Hummingbird cake with fresh cream cheese icing.'

'You're on.'

As Jenna walked back to the counter, she couldn't help but think how much she loved her job. She smiled as she stared out over the tearooms.

Almost as much as she loved Joshua Foley. He'd gone home with Amelia and Ben for a month and she missed him like crazy.

CHAPTER 5

Laura enjoyed the time they spent at Jenna's Vintage Tea Rooms. Once Petie had demolished his ice cream and looked at her with big eyes, asking for a second helping, she felt mean when she told him he'd had enough. The last thing she wanted was to have him sick when she returned him to Callie after school.

As they walked along the road to the primary school, Petie skipped along beside her, chattering nonstop. 'Now that I got rid of all the apricots, I'm fine,' he assured her a couple of times.

He had got rid of all the apricots and described it to her several times. What was it with kids and toileting? Laura shook her head as they turned the corner and headed for the crossing outside the school. Not that she'd ever know; she'd never have her own.

Sometimes, a glimmer of hope rose. Perhaps Harry would want to have a child with her, but she dismissed it. It was a ridiculous idea. Harry was in his late forties. It was time that he was thinking about easing back and thinking about retirement in a few years. He certainly wouldn't want to be saddled with a child.

Laura blinked away the surprising moisture that filled her eyes as she and Petie stood outside the school gate. What was wrong with her? She'd been so emotional the last couple of weeks, worrying that Harry's aloofness was because he didn't want to be with her anymore, which was crazy. They were planning to build a house together, for goodness' sake. He was just busy with work, and she was overtired because she had picked up a few extra shifts at the hospital. It would be good when the new nurse started. Laura knew she would prefer just to be in the maternity section, but they had been so short-staffed, she had done shifts in emergency as well as the aged-care ward over the past couple of weeks, and that was why she had been more tired than usual. She covered her mouth as she yawned. Keeping Petie entertained today had added to her tiredness.

'Do you want to go and play on the swings while we wait? Do you still feel okay?'

'I'm good. I'm just hungry again.'

Laura looked at him with a smile. Her youngest nephew was growing at the rate of knots, and the older he got, the more he was starting to look like Julia.

As Petie swung himself—higher than Laura would have liked—the musical tones of the bell sounded across the playground. The couple of times Laura had picked up her nephews, she had been pleasantly surprised by the peaceful sound of the music. The song varied every week, and she sometimes heard it as it drifted on the wind down to the hospital.

Callie had mentioned that Kimberley Riordan had suggested the music and it certainly added to the ambience of the school.

'Come on, Petie, the bell's gone.' The children were well-behaved and came out to wait for their buses in orderly lines. The rowdy ones—Laura rolled her eyes—were Nigel and Rory as they came tearing out of a building. Unfortunately for them, their stepmother came out of the building on the opposite side of the quadrangle at the same time. Callie lifted one finger, and Rory and Nigel came to a sudden stop, put their bags on their backs, and walked quietly over to the fence.

'Petie,' Laura called. 'Time to meet Mum.'

'Hi guys, did you have a good day?' Laura asked when she and Pete joined Nigel and Rory at the fence.

'Sure did, Aunty Laura. We're doing another drama production.'

Laura chuckled. The performance of the nativity play before Christmas, written by Rory and Nigel, had almost brought the house down. For a week or two afterwards, everyone was talking about their performance in the play. Their farting donkey had made them a talking point of the town.

'That sounds good. What's this one about?' Laura asked.

'This one's going to be about the history of Augathella, and it's going to have bushrangers in it,' Nigel said.

'Were there bushrangers way out here?' she asked. 'I've heard about them. We didn't have bushrangers in New Zealand.'

'You'll have to tell us about New Zealand one day, Aunty Laura. I'd like to go there,' Nigel said.

'Maybe Mum and Dad can take you for a holiday there one day, and I can come and show you around.'

A pang of sadness hit Laura. If Harry's demeanour didn't improve, maybe she was going to have to think about leaving Augathella. He had been almost dismissive of her this morning when she said goodbye. Then again, she was being unfair. Maybe he was preoccupied with something. She didn't even know the month his wife had passed away. Maybe it was the anniversary or something like that.

She needed to talk to him. Yes, she would cook a nice dinner and try to have a chat with Harry tonight.

Callie joined them, her keys in her hand. 'Hey, Petie-boy, how's that tummy been today?'

Laura chuckled. 'Well, Mum, that tummy

has seen lots of ice cream and a huge lunch.'

'And I haven't even spewed or run to the toilet once,' Petie interrupted.

'Too much information,' Rory said.

'Thanks so much for having Petie for the day, Laura.' Callie held her hand out to Petie. 'I appreciate it.'

'When's Braden back?' Laura asked.

'He'll be back tonight. He said he was going to a local cattlemen's meeting on the way home, but I'm not sure what will happen now the pub's closed.'

'I wonder how long it will be closed for? Emily and Luke were hoping to have their reception there. It's put a spoke in their plans.'

'Apparently there's a sign up on the pub door saying it's closed for three weeks.'

'Oh, yes. I've heard that too. And there's a rumour it's been sold.'

'Gosh, what are we going to do without the

pub for three weeks? There's nowhere to eat out apart from the pub. At night, that is.'

'Plus, there were a few functions booked. I don't know what will happen there. We'll have to talk to Jenna about opening up for tea.'

Callie chuckled. 'I think Jenna works hard enough. I guess we'll all be eating at home. Maybe a few barbecues around the place.'

'I know,' Laura said. 'I'll talk to Harry. We haven't had you guys over for ages. How about we have a barbeque on the weekend?'

Maybe that would get Harry out of whatever funk he was in, Laura thought.

'That sounds good to me,' Pete chimed in. 'Mum, Aunty Laura wants to take us to New Zealand for a holiday.'

Laura shook her head. 'No, that's not what I said, Petie. I said maybe Mum and Dad could take you there *one* day, and if they did, I'd come along. Anyway, Callie, I'll hand this young gentleman into your care. Now I'm going to head off and have coffee with Jenny Riley.'

Callie reached over and hugged Laura. 'Thanks so much, Laura. You were a lifesaver for the school today. We can't wait for our new teacher to arrive and we'll have an extra person on staff. I'll talk to Braden about getting together, but it sounds good to me.'

Laura nodded and pulled a face. 'I'd better check with Harry too. Who knows what he's got planned for this weekend.'

Laura decided to take her car home and then walk to Jenny Riley's house. It wasn't far from their rented place, and she could use the exercise to clear the cotton wool from her head. She knew she was worrying too much about Harry, but she had always been a worrier. Her experience with her first husband had left her insecure, and she was super-receptive and sensitive to mood changes.

She adored Harry, and they'd had a wonderful year together, but she wondered whether he was beginning to have regrets. The walk would clear her head, and *maybe* tonight, when they sat down to dinner, she would talk to him.

Maybe not, because she was scared of what he might say.

Jenny was in the front garden pruning her rose bushes when Laura turned the corner. She looked up with a smile and waved. They had become good friends over the last twelve months, serving on a couple of committees together, and even though Jenny was fifteen years older than Laura, they had a lot of common interests.

Age didn't matter with friendships, and Laura had found that to be true in Augathella, where everyone pulled together.

'Hey Laura, I was just about to go in and

put the kettle on. Ready for a cuppa?'

'I'd love one.'

Jenny glanced down at her watch. 'Actually, seeing it's close enough to five, how about a wine on the veranda? It's going to be a beautiful sunset.'

'Where's Tom?' Laura asked.

'He went out to Ben's place this morning. Ben and Amelia are away, and he's doing some work on the back of the house.'

'I heard some hammering as I walked past, but I didn't see Tom or his ute.'

Jenny laughed. 'Maybe he's gone for a beer.'

'The pub's shut.'

'Oh, I didn't know that.'

'Callie was just saying that there's a note on the door that it's closed for three weeks. She heard it's been sold.'

'Wow, that went through in secret. I don't

think many people in town know. I certainly haven't heard anything. I guess Tom's not there then; maybe he's gone down to the bowling club. Anyway, no matter. Come on in, and I'll pop a bottle open.'

A few minutes later, they were both sitting in the comfortable Papasan chairs on Jenny's veranda. Laura took a deep breath, even though it was heading into autumn, and summer had taken away the soft greens of Jenny's garden, it was still pretty. Several of her native trees were in flower, and her fruit trees had beautiful glossy green leaves. Her lawn was manicured, and Laura sighed with pleasure. 'Your garden is so beautiful. I honestly don't know how you keep the water up to it and how green it always looks.'

Jenny beamed. 'I love my garden. It gives me a lot of peace. If I'm ever worried about anything, I'll always come out and sit out here.

Not only the trees and shrubs but the view out over the paddocks too. Even though they're dry and dusty, it's still a beautiful sight.'

They sat there quietly and watched as the sun lowered, the sky changing from bright blue until the setting sun picked up the few clouds along the horizon behind the mountains and a pattern of silver and gold edged the soft apricot.

Laura sighed, and Jenny looked at her curiously.

'You don't seem yourself, Laura. Is everything okay? You're not off-colour, are you?'

'No, and I hope I won't be. I've been looking after Petie all day. He had a tummy ache from eating too many apricots, Callie suspected, and he was sick last night. So, she asked me if I could have him for the day because Braden is away.'

'And is he okay now?'

'Okay? The little terror demolished two bowls of ice cream and a massive lunch, and he was still okay when I handed him over to Callie an hour or so ago.'

'Trust me, all kids are the same. They never know when to stop. Every time Ben went to a birthday party when he was growing up, I could guarantee that he vomited when he got home because he used to eat everything that was put in front of him.'

'I hope he's better now he's grown up.' Laura smiled.

'He is, and I often wonder whether his kids will do it to him.'

'How's their new bub going?'

'Beautiful. The perfect baby. It's wonderful being a grandma.'

Jenny was silent, and Laura bit her lip. Her main regret in life was that she never had children, and unbidden tears filled her eyes.

Jenny looked at her with a frown and took Laura's hand. 'Laura, what's wrong? Did I say something to upset you? Are you okay?'

'No, I'm just being a bit maudlin, thinking back on my life. I made a wrong choice at the beginning; my first husband—my ex—wasn't a very nice man, but I persevered for as long as I could. I had a miscarriage not long before I left him, and New Zealand, and I guess now, I'll always regret not having children.'

'It's not too late now,' Jenny said. 'How old are you, Laura?'

'Oh yes, it is. I'm thirty-eight. And Harry's heading for fifty.'

'Doesn't stop it happening,' Jenny said.

'I know but we've not discussed it.'

'Please know that whatever we talk about here is confidential. You know I wouldn't say anything to anyone else.'

'You're a good friend, Jenny. I appreciate

it.'

'How about another wine?' Jenny said.

'No, thanks,' Laura sighed. 'I'd better get home and get some dinner on. I've had three days off work. It's been really nice. I've enjoyed cooking each night. Which reminds me, I went down the street today, and the butcher's got a closed sign on it too.'

'The butcher? What's happening in town?' Jenny frowned.

'I don't know. Have you seen the new buildings near Meat Ant Park?'

'I have. No one seems to know what's going in there.'

'Petie and I went past today, and a truck pulled up, and I was talking to a young woman.' Laura quickly relayed the conversation.

'Interesting. I'll have to go for a walk tomorrow and have a chat around and see if anyone knows what's happening.'

Laura shrugged. 'Whatever is, the town is changing.'

CHAPTER 6

'That was a lovely welcome from Laura and Petie,' Rosie said.

'Early days yet, don't get too excited. I've done a lot of reading through the Augathella Facebook groups and had a look at the history of the region.'

'I know what you've been doing for the last two months. It's good to do some research. I hope we can make a good life. It's very different to back home, isn't it?'

'It is, but we're here with all the people who have the same philosophy as us. They want to make a difference, and we picked a pretty little place to do it. And, my dear, you have your cattle property. Are you excited?'

'Am I excited? I'm beside myself. I can't wait to go out there and see it. I was talking to the builder on the phone when you were at the rest stop, and he said it's almost ready.'

'Almost, almost,' Rosie said.

'The kitchen and the bathrooms have been finished. All of the paving around the house has been done, and he just has to get the power connected and put on the front and back doors.'

'I can't believe you won't let me see the photo,' she said.

'No, I want it to be a wonderful surprise for you.'

'It's exciting, isn't it?' They walked along and looked at the shed that was the culmination of Greg's dreams. They had decided, in the end, that they would all be shareholders in the general store business. Gemma's hairdressing salon was next door at the front of the storage shed, and Rosie had agreed to work in the store with Greg as his assistant manager.

'It's all worked out well. Don't worry, Lex, it'll be fine.' None of them had been surprised or disappointed when Rob and Suzanne had decided not to join them. Rosie had never thought they would when the group chose the outback move. They were happy with their business, and their home in the city. Rob had retired and invested the money and agreed to help them all with their investments, and the real estate purchases. They intended travelling, and Rosie had been sad to hear that their children were staying with their grandparents while Rob and Suzanne were away.

When she and Lex had children—and she knew Chloe and Greg would be the same—they would be close to their children and they would do everything together.

'You off dreaming again, Rosie-girl? What are you thinking about?'

'Nothing important. Well, it is important, but nothing important for today.' She reached out and held his hand. 'Come on. Let's go and look at this store.' She turned as they walked along the path, already edged by a pretty flower garden. The landscapers from Charleville had done a great job. They were working on the houses that the other couples had built in town, and they were putting some gardens in ready for Rosie and Lex's small farm that they had bought only five kilometres out of town.

'How far behind us do you think the others are?' she said.

'I was talking to them after the other phone call. Greg and Chloe are about half an hour behind us and the others are not far behind.'

'Shall we wait here, and we'll all go out to look at our farm together? What do you think?'

Lex agreed. 'We do everything together. Big celebration tonight, I think. It was a great idea of Greg to put that entertainment area at the back of the storage shed and hire it out for functions.'

Rosie screwed up her face. 'The town does seem rather small. Do you think we've overcapitalised, Lex?'

'No, I'm going with Chloe's feelings. We're here to make a difference, and from what you were saying, the town has been growing, and lots of young people are moving in. I think with what we're doing, there might be a little bit more of an increase in population.'

'I think so too, sweetie. I'm so excited.' When they were almost to the back of the building, Lex stopped and put his arms around Rosie. She looked up at him and held his gaze as love surged through her. He lowered his head and their lips met in a gentle kiss. 'Are you happy, darling?' he murmured against her mouth.

'I am. No regrets. And I'm sure there won't be any,' she said. 'Now let's go and look at our store.'

CHAPTER 7

The next day

Rosie and Lex had a good look inside the first building the next morning. They'd spent their first night in town in a double swag in the other shed.

'I can't believe that the shopfitters have got this all set up already. It's absolutely beautiful, isn't it, Lex?' Rosie said. 'I think Greg is going to be very happy, but I've got a lot to learn.'

'How do you think you'll go helping him as assistant manager?' Lex asked. 'Are you sure you want to do that?'

'No, I'll be fine here, working with Greg part-time, but I've got some other ideas for things I want to do—maybe start some classes for people from the aged-care facility or work with the children at the primary school, just something to give back to this community that's going to be our new home. Like the small villages where we grew up.'

'You're a good person, Rosie.'

'Shall we look at the second shed?' As they stepped out the back and walked to the second shed, which was set up as a storage facility with the function area on the back, the rumble of a truck coming down the road reached them.

'Do you think that's the others?' Rosie said excitedly.

'Sounds like it.'

She hurried down the path through the pretty gardens where the flowers were in bud. The sprinklers had come on automatically through the night, and the grass was green and lush.

'It is! It's Chloe and Greg.' Rosie jumped up and down, then skipped out to the footpath and waited for the truck to pull up behind theirs.

Chloe jumped out straight away and raced

over to Rosie, hugging her. 'Oh, I love this place already. How beautiful is the landscape? It's so different from what I imagined. It's green and soft and gentle.'

Rosie chuckled. 'Yes, I thought so too. Did you see those pretty silver trees lining the road after Charleville?'

'I did, and I saw lots of interesting red dirt roads heading down to properties. I can't wait to explore this region.'

Greg climbed out of the driver's side and walked around the front of the truck. 'We're going to be too busy to do any exploring for a while, Chloe. Have you had a look inside, yet guys?'

Lex nodded. 'Sure have. We slept in the storage area last night.' He reached over and shook Greg's hand, and then Chloe kissed Lex on the cheek.

'Where are the others?' Rosie asked. 'Are

they far behind?'

'No, Gemma and Peter stopped for fuel at the turnoff, and Mick and Leah are only about ten minutes behind us in their car.'

'We've only had a quick look in the first shed, but it's great. I didn't know you were getting it lined, Greg. It looks fantastic.'

Greg looked a bit embarrassed. 'Did you see the flying fox I put in?'

'Flying fox?'

'Yeah. I just love that store at Maleny, the old department store. It's got the original flying fox in it. We can just use it for messages or something when you're up in the office, Rosie.'

'Better than texting,' she answered.

Chloe linked her arm with Rosie's, and they walked out to the footpath as Peter and Gemma got out of the third truck. Leah and Mick's four-wheel-drive came around the corner and parked behind the three trucks.

'They look pretty good together, don't they? It's the first time the trucks have been in a line since we left Brisbane,' Chloe said.

'I can't believe how quickly you all caught up to us.'

Leah laughed. 'We were so excited. We just wanted to get here, so we decided to drive through the night. That's how we got here early.'

'We did stop in Charleville for a while and had a look around.'

'Pete, how'd you go driving the truck?' Lex asked.

Pete had only got his light rigid license a couple of weeks before they came away. 'Easy as.' He chuckled and looked down at Gemma. 'I even commented to Gem that I'd like to be a truck driver in a new life.'

Lex and Rosie looked at each other and burst out laughing.

'Exactly the same thing Lex said. Maybe we've got a couple of truckies here,' Rosie said.

'Hey, that's not a bad idea because rather than getting a freight company to bring our stock from Brisbane, we've got the trucks, so we can go and get it.'

Pete grinned. 'We can be truckies.'

'Don't get carried away, you pair, because it won't only be Brisbane,' Chloe said. 'Greg and I were talking on the way out, and we really want to keep the content of the department store as Australian as we can. We can have a girls' trip around some small towns and purchase local products. Knitting and crochet, pottery and woodwork and things like that once we get settled. What do you think, girls?'

Gemma nodded. 'Yeah, that would be good, but I'm going to be busy setting up my salon. I've got no idea how many clients I'll have because the town doesn't look anywhere near as big as I was expecting. I hope we haven't made a mistake.'

'Gemma, it'll be fine. As well as all the outlying properties, apparently there are a lot of new people moving into town. I was talking to a local lady and her nephew a short while ago, and she was telling me there are so many people coming into town that they sometimes have welcome functions at the park.'

'We could do something social in the back of the second shed. You haven't looked at it yet?' Greg asked.

'I can't wait.' Chloe said. 'Let's go and have a look.'

CHAPTER 8

Callie was staying back at school late this afternoon as the new teacher who had moved out from Brisbane was meeting her to look at the special education classroom. So it was Braden's job to pick up the boys, give them afternoon tea in town, and then pick up Callie at five o'clock.

'I'm so excited that we've got a specialist special education teacher,' Callie had said that morning as he dropped her and the two boys at school before he dropped Petie off to Prep at ten o'clock. They'd dropped the twins to Ruth on the way into town. 'Her qualifications are fabulous, and I can't wait to meet her.'

'What does her husband do? Will he be looking for work?' Braden asked.

'When I was talking to Leah on the phone, she said that her husband got a transfer out here, but I'm not sure what he does. Out here in Augathella, there isn't much to transfer to, apart from the hospital, the police station, or the school.'

Braden nodded slowly. 'Yeah, Sergeant Mitcham said he was looking at retiring shortly. Maybe he's done it on the quiet, and a new policeman is coming to town. It'll be good to have more new people in town, too.'

'Yes,' Callie agreed. 'We've got so many in the agricultural sector and some new people at that function in the park the afternoon I had the twins. It's so exciting to see the town growing.'

'We might have to hold another welcome function,' Braden said.

'Sounds like a plan, with whatever's happening with those sheds and the new houses down in Hill Street. I'll ask Leah where her husband works when I'm talking to her this afternoon.'

'Well, it's certainly not them building the new sheds, if they've both got transfers to town,' Braden commented.

Callie leaned over and kissed him. 'Come on, boys, we don't want to be late.' Rory and Nigel jumped out of each side of the car.

Braden chided Nigel. 'How many times have I told you not to get out on the roadside?'

'Sorry, Dad, I forgot. I couldn't get past Petie. He's got his leg stuck up. On purpose,' Nigel snarled. 'I looked first to see if any cars were coming.'

'Well, don't do it again; it's dangerous.'

Peter stuck out his tongue. 'I did not.'

'You did so. I was watching. You put your legs up,' Nigel yelled.

Callie rolled her eyes. 'Come on, you pair. Nigel, lose that temper before you go into class. I don't want you hassling Miss Emily. I'll see you about five, Bray.'

'Love you, Callie.'

'Love you too,' Callie said as she climbed out of the car.

Braden headed down the street towards the park. They had an hour to fill in before Perie started prep.

Petie pointed out the window. 'Dad, have you seen that truck? The one I told you about, the purple swirly one. Go up past Meat Ant Park, and you'll see them.'

Braden glanced at his watch; he had plenty of time before he had to be at Craig Wilson's property. He was looking at some cattle there today and meeting Jon Ingram out there as well.

'Mate, I've got time.' He put the indicator on and waited for some children to cross at the crossing before turning down Main Street.

'Look, it's still there' Petie said. 'And there's more! There's three of those flash trucks now.'

Braden parked a little way down from the butcher shop that had newspapers covering the front windows.

'I wonder what's happening?'

'Aunty Laura asked that the other day too. I've heard her talking to Emily about it, and there's gonna be a new butcher shop too.'

'Wow, things are changing,' Braden said.

'I like it, Dad. I think these trucks are doing special things in our town. I liked the lady.'

'I don't think they've got anything to do with the butcher, mate.'

'I bet they have. That lady was really nice.'

'Which lady was that?'

'The lady who got out of the truck. She talked to us for a long time. If the trucks are there, she might still be there,' Petie said. 'Can we go and see?'

Braden parked the Landcruiser down from

the park. 'Come on, jump out, and we'll go for a stroll.'

'Can I have a swing at the park too?'

'I suppose you can. I've got a while before I have to meet Jon. But you don't want to be late for school.'

'I hate prep with the little kids. I want to go to big school.'

Braden rolled his eyes. His sweet little Petie was turning into another Nigel. 'Next year, mate. Not long. We don't want you to grow up too quick.'

'Why not? We've got the twins now.' Petie yelled back as he raced over to the swings in the park. 'Do you want to come push me, Dad?'

'Sure.' Brayden walked over and gave the swing a solid push. 'I'm just going to suss out these trucks, mate.'

'I wonder what's inside them? Do you think there's something special in there, or do you think it's just boring stuff?' Petie asked as he made the swing go higher. 'Maybe it's a circus.'

Ever since the circus had come to town when Petie was three, he talked about it incessantly. Maybe one day it would come back, but Braden doubted very much this was a circus. He walked along the road, keeping one eye on Petie as he swung himself on the swing.

He looked at the logo on the trucks wondering if it was the name of a company or whether it was the name of some sort of church.

There was activity at the back of both sheds, so he yelled at Petie, 'Come on, mate. I'm going down to have a look, hop off and catch me up.'

Petie soon caught up to Braden, with his eyes wide as he looked at the three trucks. 'They're much bigger than your cattle truck, Dad.'

'Sure are, mate.'

'Maybe we can go and ask them what's inside,' he said.

'I'm sure we'll find out. Come on.' Braden looked down with a smile as Petie slipped his little hand into his.

Contentment filled him as he walked along with Petie swinging their arms. Life was good, even though he and Callie might both be a bit tired with the twins.

'Good morning,' he said, as a guy walked around the side of the first shed.

'Hey there.' The man was tall with broad shoulders and a wide smile, dressed in a pair of khaki pants and a long-sleeved shirt. Braden walked over and held out his hand. 'Braden Cartwright.'

'I'm Lex Renouf. You live in town, Braden?'

'Sort of, I'm a local from birth. I've got a cattle property about thirty ks out on the old

Charleville Road.'

The guy's eyes brightened. 'I might be in touch with you, mate. I'm starting a little property close to town, but I'm a city slicker and I've got no idea what I'm doing.'

'Great to make a change. I'm happy to help. We'll have a chat when you get organised,' Braden said. He gestured with his head to the trucks. 'These your trucks?'

Lex nodded. 'Yes, there's a few of us moving to town.'

'The town's a little bit intrigued by what's happening,' Braden replied. 'Are these sheds yours? Or are you working here?'

'They're ours,' Lex said. 'Come round the back and meet the others, and I'll show you what we're doing.'

Petie's eyes were wide as they walked around, Braden still holding his hand. There was a small area behind the first and largest building—they were more than the sheds he'd thought—with some tables and chairs and an outdoor kitchen. At the back of the smaller building, was a huge outdoor entertainment area with a wood fire, a barbecue, and a lot of furniture that was waiting to be arranged.

'Looks interesting,' Braden commented.

'Yes, we're hoping it'll all work out for us. Augathella's a little bit smaller than we thought, but it was the town we chose to move to. Come and I'll introduce you to the others. Would you like a cup of tea? We were about to take a break. We've been unloading the trucks since we arrived.' The English accent was very pronounced and Braden wondered if they'd emigrated from the UK to Augathella. He glanced at his watch. 'Won't say no to that. I just have to drop my boy at school before ten.'

As he spoke, a woman came out of the second shed, carrying a small box.

She smiled as she spotted them. 'Hello, Petie.'

'Hello, Rosie,' Petie said.

'Hi, I met your son yesterday. I'm Rosie, Lex's wife. I see you've already met him.' Three other couples walked out of the shed carrying empty boxes, and Braden wondered what was going on as they flattened them and added them to a pile of cardboard.

'Guys, come and meet Braden,' Lex said. 'He's a local cattle farmer. I'll be picking his brains, I'm sure.'

Braden was introduced to Leah and Mick first. He held out his hand and Mick's grip was firm.

'Good to meet you, Braden,' Mick said. 'I've been transferred here as the new police sergeant.'

'Congratulations. I heard old Sarge was thinking of retiring.' He turned back to Leah.

'Are you the new teacher at the school?'

'I am,' she said. 'I've got a meeting there this afternoon.'

Braden smiled. 'I know. With Callie Cartwright, my wife. She's looking forward to meeting you.'

'Oh, that's wonderful. And this is Petie. Do you have any brothers and sisters, Petie?' Leah crouched down and spoke to him face-to-face.

'I have two big brothers, Rory and Nigel, and a little brother and a little sister. They're twins, and they're babies, and really noisy, and Mum and Dad are always complaining that they don't get enough sleep.'

Braden chuckled. 'Yes, we're in that first six months stage when sleep is very precious when it does happen.'

'Something to look forward to when we start a family.' Mick grinned and gestured to the two couples who joined them, but before he could introduce them, Petie tugged on Braden's arm.

'Excuse me, Dad? Can I go and play outside?' He pulled his favourite metal car out of his pocket.

'As long as you don't go out the front. And watch out for snakes.'

'Okay, I will.' Petie headed off to a pile of dirt near the side fence.

'Lovely manners,' Leah commented.

'Most of the time. We've got good kids.'

Leah smiled. 'This is Gemma and Peter, and Chloe and Greg.

'Welcome to town,' Braden said as he shook hands with both men and smiled at the women.

'Peter's managing the store,' Mick added.

'The store?'

'We haven't put the sign up yet, but we're opening a department store in the other building,' Peter replied.

Braden whistled. 'Holy heck, that's a big step for all you guys. But great for our town.'

'Yes, we're a bit worried that maybe we've overcapitalised considering the size of the town, but nothing ventured, nothing gained, is our motto.'

'Don't worry, there's a fair-sized population on the outlying properties, and I know they'll be grateful not to have to drive to Charleville.' Braden chuckled. 'When I saw "New Life" on your truck, I thought you might've been setting up a church here.'

'Oh gosh, no,' Chloe said. 'We've come here to start our new life in the country.'

'You'll certainly make an impact on the town with the new store. What's this building for?'

'It's a storage shed, and at the back, we're opening an indoor and outdoor entertainment and function centre. If a band comes to town or if someone wants to get married or hold a party, we figured the town could use a venue,' Greg said. 'We did some research on the climate when we chose Augathella, and realised the heat would restrict a lot of outdoor functions.'

'We do have the pub, but even though it's a bit small, it's always busy. It's closed for renovations at the moment.'

Greg nodded and glanced at the others. 'Yes, we've bought the pub too. We're refurbishing that, and we're hoping to get it open in the next month or so.'

'You bought the pub too,' Braden exclaimed, his eyes wide. Who were these people—a fleet of trucks, two big sheds, and they'd bought the pub as well? 'Wow, what made you choose our town? Do you have connections here?'

'No, we don't.' Chloe looked sheepish.

'Well, when we all decided to move west, we pulled out a map and all put our fingers on it, and Augathella was the place we picked.'

'I'm pleased you chose us. So, hang on, are you building those new houses in Hill Street too?' he asked.

Chloe nodded. 'Yes, we bought up half a dozen empty houses. We made sure no one was planning on moving into them, and that they didn't belong to any families. We would hate to upset the town, and we've merged each of the two blocks into one. Leah and Mick, and Gemma and Peter, and Greg and I, are moving down there when they're finished. Until then, we're going to bunk in the second shed.'

'We slept in there, last night,' Rosie said. 'It's pretty comfortable, and the guest amenities are certainly big enough for the eight of us to share for a while. Shouldn't be too long though till our farm homestead is ready.'

'Well, you're certainly busy.' Another thought struck him. 'Tell me, what about the butcher shop?'

Rosie nodded. 'Yes, we bought that too. After we chose Augathella, our partner in Brisbane had a look at what was for sale in town, and here we are. It was all Chloe's doing.'

'Well, Chloe, you're certainly the entrepreneur,' Braden said, blown away by this group of people. 'I don't think the town is going to know what's hit it. Crumbs, between the lot of you, you own more of the town than anyone. You'll be made very much welcome,' he said, smiling. 'Anyway, it's been great to meet you all and welcome again. Leah, I'll give Callie a call and organise a time for all of you to come out and visit us at *Kilcoy Station*. How would you like that?'

The girls beamed, and the guys nodded.

'That sounds fabulous. A great welcome to the community.'

***

Callie turned to her handbag as her phone beeped as she prepared the classroom for the first session of the day. The message was from Braden. '**Are you in class yet?**'

She hit speed dial and called him and he picked up straight away.

'Hi sweetie, what's up? Everything okay?'

'Yeah, everything's fine. Petie and I went to the park, and we met the people he was talking about with the "swirly" truck. There's quite a big concern happening in town. There are four couples in their group and they seem like good people. Leah, your teacher, is one of them, and her husband is the new sergeant. I mentioned that I'd speak to you and suggested that we have them all out for a barbeque on the weekend. I hope that's okay.'

'No, that's fine, as long as the twins get some sleep.'

'What about we invite Sophie and Kent, and Fallon and Jon too?'

'You must have been impressed to invite them out so soon.'

'Yeah, one of the guys is starting a small property, and he's a bit of a greenhorn. I think he'd appreciate having a couple of us to talk to.'

'Sounds good.'

'What about the others? What are they doing?'

'Lots of stories there; I'll tell you when I pick you up this afternoon. But it involves a new department store in town, the butcher shop, and would you believe they've bought the pub as well? And they're building all those houses in Hill Street.'

'Oh, my goodness, there will be some change in town. Anyway, I have to go, love; the bell's about to ring. I'll look forward to meeting them, and I'll see you this afternoon, sweetheart. Have a good day and drive safe. Bye.'

CHAPTER 9

'Another lovely welcome to town,' Rosie said to Chloe as she stocked the small kitchen in the back of the first shed. Braden had stayed for a cup of tea, and Rosie had made Petie a small milkshake. They had a great chat, found out a lot about the town, and added to their certainty that they had done the right thing.

'You're quiet today, Chloe. Are you okay?' Rosie asked.

Chloe smiled. She had something on her mind, and she was pretty sure that she was right. However, she was not going to breathe a word of it to anybody until she was certain, or before she told Greg.

'Yeah, I'm fine, just a bit tired from that trip. I'm gonna go for a wander around the street later. Do you want to come for a walk, Rosie?'

'I promised Lex we'd go out and check out our farm and see how close the house is to moving in.'

'I keep forgetting that you've got the farm out there, and we're all in town,' Chloe said. 'Okay.' She reached over and hugged her friend. 'I'm going to go for a bit of a wander now. I'll see you when you get back from your farm.'

'Who'd a thought it?' Rosie grinned and her cockney accent was strong.

'Meant to be, Rosie dear.' Chloe picked up her purse and walked out to the truck where Greg, Lex, Mick, and Peter were wrangling some extra heavy boxes to bring in. They had brought quite a bit of stock for the store in two of the trucks, and the other trucks held their furniture and personal possessions.

'I'm just going for a stroll down the street,' Chloe said.

'Okay, babe, catch you when you get back. Have fun.' Greg leaned over and kissed her.

'Don't overdo it,' she said. 'We don't have to rush to unpack.' The four men had perspiration running down their faces, and their shirts were soaked.

'We won't,' Peter said.

Chloe didn't look at the Google map on her phone as she walked. As it was such a small town, if she got lost, it didn't matter. She knew the general direction of where their houses were, but she wouldn't go down and look at them until Greg was with her.

She walked down the main street and saw the hotel on the corner with several builders' utes parked outside. The butcher shop had newspapers over the front windows.

Chloe walked past one intersection and then saw the sign for the hospital. She smiled and then turned left into the street.

***

Laura had come into the hospital to do a couple of hours over the lunch break. Harry was in Charleville at yet another meeting, and she had antenatal checks for two pregnant women who had come in at lunchtime.

She'd just finished when Helen, the receptionist from the front counter, came in. 'Are you still here, Laura?

'I am. Just finished.'

'Great, there's a young woman at the front who was hoping to visit the clinic, and I said I wasn't sure if you were here. Are you happy to see another patient?'

'Of course, not a problem. What's her name?'

'Her name is Chloe Redman.'

'Sure, just ask her to take a seat in the waiting room, and I'll be out in a moment.'

'I'll give her a patient form to fill in,' Helen

said.'

'Thank you.' Laura quickly tidied up the room. After having a wash, she made her way out to the waiting room.

'Chloe?' she said to the young woman sitting in the chair.

'Yes, I'm Chloe, thank you for seeing me.'

'Hello, I'm Sister Adnum, but please call me Laura. Come on in.'

Chloe was a stunningly beautiful young woman with black curls pulled back from her face, and her cheeks held a pretty pink flush. As she handed over the patient information form, big brown eyes looked directly at Laura as though she could see into her thoughts. A ripple of goosebumps ran down Laura's back.

'So, come on in, Chloe. Have a seat. What can I do for you?' She glanced down at the form.

'Well,' Chloe said, 'we've just moved to

town.'

'Ah, I see you live in Hill Street.'

'Yes, we will be living there. We're waiting for our house to be finished. We're camping out at the sheds we've built near the park while we wait.'

'Oh, are you with Rosie? I met her there yesterday.'

'Yes, that's me, that's us. The rest of us arrived this morning.'

'Welcome to town. Now, what can I do for you?'

'I'm pregnant,' Chloe said, and a happy smile tilted her lips.

'You're sure you're pregnant? Have you done a pregnancy test?' Laura asked.

She shook her head. 'No, I haven't, but I know I'm pregnant.'

'So, let's do a pregnancy test. I can draw blood and it will take a couple of days to come back, or if you are further along, a urine test will confirm your pregnancy today.'

'A urine test will be fine,' Chloe said calmly. 'It's just a confirmation for me so I can be sure when my husband asks for the proof.' She chuckled.

Fifteen minutes later, they were sitting back at Laura's desk.

'Well, Chloe, you were right. The urine test has confirmed your assumption.'

Laura was taken aback by the sudden tears rolling down her patient's face. 'So, were you trying to fall pregnant, or is it a surprise to you?'

The young woman dabbed at her tears and her smile widened if that was possible. 'Greg, my husband, and I have been through three rounds of IVF, and we weren't successful. I knew I had to have faith, and I was right. This is a natural pregnancy.'

'Well, we'll have to take extra special care of you, won't we?'

Chloe nodded and smiled, and her eyes held Laura's intently.

'When are you due, Laura?'

'I'm sorry? You mean, when are you due?'

Chloe shook her head. 'No, I know the day I fell pregnant. It was two months ago, so I'm due at the end of September. I thought you were pregnant?'

'No, of course I'm not.' She frowned as Chloe's gaze ran down her front and she placed a hand on her flat stomach.

'I'm sorry, Laura. I shouldn't have said anything. I'm sure you'll hear about me when you get to know the girls, but my intuition is nothing sinister. I just have this skill—I suppose you should call it—where I seem to know things. I'm sorry I blurted that out. I just got a very strong sense that you were carrying a baby.'

What a strange young woman. Perhaps she picked up the very strong sense that she would love to have a baby. Was her yearning so obvious?

'You take care of yourself, Chloe, and I'll get you to come and see Dr Higgins in the next week or so, and then I'm sure I'll see you at our clinic again in the next few weeks. Welcome to Augathella.'

CHAPTER 10

When Laura left the hospital, she called in at the small supermarket.

Harry would be tired after his meeting and the drive home, and she decided to prepare his favourite dinner. With the butcher being shut, she went straight to the back of the store and picked a small leg of lamb from the meat cabinet.

She knew Harry wouldn't be home for ages. So, she wandered along the aisles, taking more time than she usually did on her rushed weekly shopping trip. Her thoughts were churning, with that inappropriate comment that Chloe had made; there was no way she could be pregnant.

Laura found rosemary and quince gourmet gravy and added it to her basket. Then she walked down the confectionery aisle, added a small box of chocolates and then headed back to the cold section and picked out a frozen cheesecake. Loving cooking, she didn't often buy pre-packaged food, but tonight the thought of cooking made her feel even more tired. It wouldn't hurt them to have a Sara-Lee cheesecake and packet gravy. It would give her time to sit down and put her feet up when she got home. She was back at work tomorrow, so an easy night watching a movie with Harry would be nice.

Debbie Allen, one of the regular cashiers at the supermarket, smiled at her as she unloaded her basket onto the counter.

'Hi Laura, how are you. Day off?'

'Hello, Debbie. Sort of, I've had a couple of days off, but I had to go into the clinic for a couple of hours this morning.'

'I saw you walk past across the road to the park with young Petie yesterday. Is he okay? He's not had a relapse, has he?' The whole town had pulled together last year when Petie had had a serious head injury.

'He's fine. He had a bit of an upset tummy, so I offered to look after him for Callie. We had a lovely day.'

'He's a sweet child, that miracle boy. Some of the things that he and those boys get up to and some of the things Peter comes out with, I laugh every time Callie brings him in here. I hope the twins are a bit quieter. You're their aunt, aren't you?' Debbie asked with a frown.

'Yes, I am. I don't know if you knew Julia, Braden's first wife and their mum. She was my sister.'

'I did. She was a beautiful girl.'

'Thank you. Anyway, I better get home and get this leg of lamb in the oven.'

'Looks like a special tea tonight. Birthday?'

'No, just a roast dinner.'

'I'll see you next time. Laura, don't work

too hard.'

Laura breathed deeply as she walked home. The weather was still warm, and the air was dry, but despite the climate being so different to what she was used to, she still loved living here. She pushed aside her worries about Harry, but she would sit down and have a chat with him tonight.

And Chloe's strange words wouldn't leave her.

CHAPTER 11

Later that day

Rosie's excitement was bubbling over so much she didn't know if she could handle it as she stood in the middle of the huge storage shed and twirled around, looking at the hundreds and hundreds and hundreds of unopened boxes that still filled the space. They had done it—the first part of the dream was happening.

Chloe wandered over with Gemma. 'Are you all right there, Rosie? You look like you're going to burst.'

Rosie grabbed Chloe's shoulders and hugged her, then turned to Gemma and hugged her as well. 'I am just so happy.'

She knew when she got excited, her Cockney accent became more pronounced, and Chloe and Gemma smiled.

'Slow down, you're hard to understand sometimes, girlfriend.'

'I'm so excited. I can't believe we've done this. We're in a new town. The first stock has been unpacked. And while we've got to unpack the rest, I think we need to get onto the community Facebook page and start advertising for some young people to come and help us. What do you think, Chloe?'

'I think that's a great idea, but we have to wait until the rest of the shelves come down from Longreach tomorrow. The shop fitter is coming back to put the shelves for the goods in the storage area, and then we can get it all unpacked. He's going to do the shelves in the aisles of this front part for us first. It will give us a lot more room while we're camping here.'

'What about the third other shed they're planning to build?' Gemma asked. 'We still haven't completely decided what to do with that one.'

'I think the boys are still talking about it, but I'm pretty sure they're going to turn it into a car showroom, and Mick says boats are a must.'

'Why on earth would anyone need a boat out here?' Leah asked.

Chloe laughed. 'You're such a coastie, Leah. There *is* a river and there are lots of big dams around. We'll have to take you yabby fishing.'

'Good, I love fishing.'

'Maybe we need to give that shed a bit more thought,' Rosie said. 'We've got enough work to keep us going for a while. How are the guys going with the pub?'

'They've got onto this great builder from Tambo,' Chloe said.

'Tambo, that's a funny name,' Rosie commented.

'Yeah, it's a cute little town just up the way

and it's really progressive. There's an art gallery there and a couple of smaller galleries plus a community centre and three or four pubs. It's only a small town. I don't think it's as big as our town.'

'I like the sound of that, *our* town.' Rosie smiled.

'Anyway, the pub is going well. He reckons he can have it open again in three weeks. I guess the community hasn't been happy with losing their watering hole,' Chloe said.

'How about,' Rosie put her head on the side, 'while the pub is being refurbished, how hard would it be to move the pub to the shed next door while we work on this one?'

'But we wouldn't have a license to sell alcohol.'

'We could use the licence for the pub; we own the pub and the licence. We could just move the premises while it's being refurbished.

I can't see a problem with that. I'll run it by the guys later and make some inquiries. I'll ring the council and everything or whoever I have to ring—maybe a liquor board.'

'Sounds good to me. Robert, the butcher who the guys hired to run the shop, has had a good look around, and there's hardly anything that needs doing down there. We're just going to order some gourmet products from Brisbane and get it flown out so we've got some different stuff to the normal cuts of beef and lamb and chicken.'

'And the new houses are going well,' Leah said. 'They've found another six that they're going to refurbish.'

'Do we really have enough time to do all this?' Chloe said.

'Don't you start doubting now; this was all your idea, and it was the most wonderful idea.'

'I still can't believe we pulled it off in just a

few short months.' Gemma's eyes were wide as she shook her head. 'It's incredible how everything is going to plan.'

'And Rob was a great help. And yes, the universe is looking out for us. I always knew it would,' Chloe said. 'I had no doubt, and I think if we stay positive and keep in mind our reasons for what we're doing, it's going to be absolutely wonderful. Give it six months and then we'll see what the town looks like.'

'The only thing I'm worried about,' Rosie said with a frown, 'is that the locals might see us as interlopers. I mean, I imagine a lot of people would've lived here most of their lives, and here comes the eight of us bowling into town, buying the pub, buying the butcher shop, and changing things that they've always had.'

'But look what we're doing,' Leah said. 'We're starting new facilities, and we're offering more in the existing businesses. And we'll create jobs for the locals too.'

'It's hard with the pub being renovated, we sort of can't go anywhere and meet anyone,' Gemma said.

Rosie answered quickly. 'Lex is organising that with Braden Cartwright. He was going to talk to the guys about it this afternoon. Have some sort of function here. But I guess if we go with the idea of having a temporary pub, we can have the complimentary welcome do to start with and invite the town, and then have the pub open here for the next two or three weeks. We'd get to know a lot of people that way.'

'See, we're not just coming in and taking over the town; we're coming in and providing lots of services.'

'Well, let's just take it easy and wait and see that we don't put a step wrong.' Chloe's eyes were bright and her voice was full of confidence. 'I think it's time we grabbed our men, and went down and had a look at our new houses.'

CHAPTER 12

Laura was sitting on the back patio with a drink when she heard the front door open. She'd put a wine glass out for Harry too, and had a bottle cooling in an ice cooler on the table, along with a small tray of nibbles. She stood and went to the sliding door and called out, 'I'm out the back, Harry. I've got a wine ready for you.'

'Thanks, love. I'll be a minute. I want to take a quick shower. I feel like I've got the whole of Charleville Hospital on me today; it's been a busy couple of days.'

'I missed you,' she said. Harry simply smiled as he headed for the bathroom.

Laura sat out there for ten minutes and waited, and eventually, Harry came out, his damp hair slicked back, looking casual in a pair of shorts and a short-sleeved T-shirt. He reached over and kissed her cheek.

'You look refreshed and rested,' he said.

'I am, even though Petie nearly wore me out yesterday. And then Deb called me into the hospital today for a couple of hours.'

Harry chuckled. 'How is the little monkey?'

'He's a beautiful boy.'

'I think you have a soft spot for your almost youngest nephew, not forgetting Munro.'

'I didn't see the twins. They were already at Ruth's when I met Callie and Petie yesterday morning. But I did see Rory and Nigel in the afternoon. They were full of beans as usual too.'

Harry sat back and closed his eyes as Laura poured his glass of wine. She put it on the coaster in front of him and sat back, letting him rest.

A lazy late summer afternoon with only the soothing drone of a mower two or three doors, and the occasional bird squawking down the back in the thicket of bush broke the comfortable silence.

Eventually, Harry stretched and reached for his wine. 'Thank you. This will go down well.'

'A busy couple of days?'

'Not so much bad as busy. The meeting with the remote specialists yesterday was good, but the meeting with the hospital board at Charleville today was stressful. I managed to have about three wins.'

'That's good.' Laura looked at him intently. 'No more news about our maternity ward closing again?'

'No, we managed to come to an agreement, and we've been given a three-month reprieve. But we need to have more women coming through for their antenatal check-ups to make them realise it's a viable service.'

Laura sighed. 'I know they think about the money. We've got the staffing and the board, and we have a small community who would like to see their local hospital retain its services.'

'If the board down in Charleville gets their way, the whole hospital will become an aged-care facility. I could see the town, in a few years, not even having a doctor in it, to be truthful.'

'But you can't expect people to travel eighty kilometres for medical help.'

Harry shrugged. 'It's the way things are going. They can't get enough staff out here; they can't get doctors.'

'Okay, let's talk about something nice. You've been doing this stuff all day. You don't want to spend the evening talking about politics and hospitals and medical services.'

'True. I've been thinking, Laura. Maybe we should go away for a week or even a couple of days next time we both have time off at the same time.'

'That would be nice. Where would we go? Maybe we could fly somewhere from Charleville. Do something really exciting.'

'Do you think we're in a bit of a rut?' Harry's tone was serious, and a quiver of uncertainty ran through Laura.

'Oh no, I didn't mean that,' she said. 'I didn't think we were in a rut at all. Do you?' she asked carefully.

Harry was silent for a moment, but he held her gaze. Eventually, he shook his head. 'No, of course I don't.' As soon as he spoke, he stood up and finished the wine that was in his glass. 'I'm going to go and put the news on. Are you going to come inside shortly?'

'Yes, I have to come in and turn the vegetables over.'

'Smells good, love,' he said. 'I'll see you inside.'

Laura sat out there for a moment and couldn't help the tears prickling in her eyes. Somehow, their closeness seemed to have lessened over the past few months. She hadn't noticed it at first; they were only little things. But now, Harry didn't seem as invested in their relationship as he had been twelve months ago.

She took a deep breath and stood up. She was strong; she had been through the loss of a relationship before, and at that time it had been exacerbated by the loss of their child, their stillborn baby. She closed her eyes to stop tears from forming, realising she had to pull herself together. She had a lot to be thankful for. She couldn't expect Harry to be Romeo; for goodness' sake, he was not far off fifty. He'd had a long and happy first marriage, and they had been together for only a little while. They had settled into a relationship like a comfortable pair of shoes, and that's what she had to be happy with.

'Thank you,' Harry said as he picked up the napkin that Laura had placed in the centre of the table, and dabbed his mouth. 'That was beautiful. Thank you, Laura. It's exactly what I needed.' As well as eating the roast lamb, baked vegetables, and a healthy-sized piece of cheesecake, Harry drank half the bottle of wine.

She smiled as some of the tension that had built over the past two days left her as he held her gaze, her limbs loose and her confidence building. That silly young woman at the hospital had really unsettled her for a while. 'Harry, can I ask you something?'

'Of course, you can.' He stood and turned to the small living room adjacent to the kitchen. 'Come and sit with me.'

'Doesn't matter.'

'Come on. What did you want to ask me?'

Laura's confidence fled. She didn't want to

ask Harry outright whether he was a little bit over having her as a new partner because she knew he was honest and would tell the truth, and she didn't want to hear it.

'Okay, I've heard about this fantastic new series on Netflix, and I was hoping you'd watch it with me tonight. Maybe the first or second episodes. We could snuggle up on the couch,' she suggested. 'I'll leave the dishes till the morning. It's my last day off.'

Harry shook his head. 'I'm sorry, love. I'm too tired to watch a series. I'm going to go to bed as soon as I help you clear the kitchen, but you stay up and watch your show. I'll just go to bed and get some sleep.'

##

Laura yawned as she switched the television off. She had enjoyed the first two episodes of the new series and had smiled a couple of times when she heard Harry's gentle snores coming from their bedroom.

The series episodes had been a little bit sad, and she wiped away a couple of tears. However, the end of the second episode left her with a smile on her face, and she was heading off to bed feeling a little bit happier.

Even though Harry hadn't watched the movie with her, they'd had a lovely evening before he went to bed.

She reached over and picked up the cushion, holding it against her as she walked to the end of the lounge to reposition them. Even though it was a little rented cottage, Laura had added lots of homely touches. She had done an interior design course when she had been in New Zealand and enjoyed having a nice space to live in. She frowned as the cushion moved; her breast was tender. She placed the cushion carefully on the end of the three-seater sofa, moved her fingers along the soft tissue and felt around. There was no doubt about it. Her right breast was tender. Her mouth dried. Her aunt had breast cancer when she was in her forties, but Laura had taken the test and wasn't carrying the gene.

Still, it would be worth going to Charleville and having a mammogram. She moved her fingers gently and slowly over to her left breast and frowned when it was tender too. It was the sort of tenderness that she used to have when she was in her teens when her period was due.

She sat on the lounge and thought for a moment, and suddenly a cold feeling ran through her as Chloe's question came back to her, quickly followed by a gush of joy.

Surely she couldn't be pregnant. They used contraception. No, she couldn't be.

There was only one way to check.

But there was no way she was going to do a pregnancy test at the hospital on her day off or buy one from the local pharmacy, so she would go down to Charleville and do it.

Her thoughts went rapidly around her head as she walked down the hallway to the bedroom. Harry's gentle snores were still puffing away. She climbed into bed and lay beside him with her eyes wide open. There was a tight muscle twinge down in her lower belly like she'd had early in her first pregnancy. Laura moved her hand down gently on her nightie, feeling the firmness at the base of her stomach.

Surely not? Oh, my God, what was Harry going to say just when she was wondering whether he was ready to end their relationship?

She *could* be pregnant, but the worry was superseded by the happiness that flooded through her. She knew Harry would do the right thing by her, even if they weren't a couple anymore. And if she was pregnant, it would mean that she'd have the baby she'd always wanted.

Laura's eyes closed, and she went to sleep with a smile on her face.

CHAPTER 13

Laura sat in the new coffee shop near the central intersection of the main street in Charleville as she worked up her courage. Her trip to Charleville had been timely as Harry had a delivery to pick up from the hospital there, and she offered to get it while she was in town.

'Not like you to go to Charleville, Laura,' he asked with a smile. 'What are you up to down there?'

'I just thought I'd like to get a couple of new things for the house. I need a vase for the kitchen. Jenny gives me so many flowers; I'd like to have a bigger vase to put on the kitchen table.'

Harry nodded. 'Well, you have a lovely day.' He gave her an absent-minded kiss on the cheek and headed out to the car to go to work at the hospital. He was certainly preoccupied, and she tried not to put too much emphasis on the cause of his preoccupation being their relationship.

He was very professional and rarely talked about any of the issues he faced at the hospital, but she knew it was a difficult job.

She went to one of the chemists in town and lingered outside until it was almost empty. She walked in, and unfortunately, when she picked up the pregnancy kit at the front counter, the woman looked at her.

'Oh, you're the midwife at the hospital at Augathella. I suppose you need this for some of the young women up there.'

Laura looked at her and nodded. She didn't want to get into a conversation about what she was buying. She paid for it and quickly added a few other things to her purchase so it didn't look too obvious that's what she came in for.

She made her way to the coffee shop, and now she was sitting there with a latte and a slice of cake that tasted like straw.

Would she do it here or would she do it at home?

No, she would do it here. Finishing off her coffee and pushing the half-eaten cake away, Laura stood and made her way out to the street.

There was a block of public amenities at the back of the park, and she knew that they were clean. Taking a deep breath, she picked her bag up and headed down the street.

***

Harry had a quiet day at the hospital. He'd seen a couple of patients from the aged-care wing, and there had been a student from the primary school with a sprained ankle. Callie had brought the young boy in before his parents arrived, and Harry had him X-rayed, bandaged, and in the waiting room before they arrived;

they had given their permission over the phone as they lived on a property an hour out of town.

'How are you, Callie?' he asked. 'How are you going with those twins of yours? Laura keeps me in the loop. She says they're growing fast.'

'Yes, they are.'

'We must get together,' Harry said.

'Braden and I are thinking about having a barbecue at our place to welcome some of the new people in town. You and Laura would be most welcome to come out.'

'Sounds good.'

'I'll keep in touch.'

'I did wonder what was going on in town,' he said. 'Laura mentioned this morning that she met a couple while I was away. So, you're back at work, Callie? How are you coping? Not too tired? You've got a big load.'

'I have, but Braden is wonderful, so I'm

very good. How about you, Harry?' she said. 'I'm not asking as a doctor; I'm asking as a friend.'

He chuckled. 'I'm good. Just a bit preoccupied.'

'Everything okay?'

'Everything is really okay; I've just got a bit on my mind,' he said.

'Well, if you ever need anyone to chat to, I'm sure Laura is there for you. But if you need to talk about anything else, I think we're close enough friends, and you and Braden are good mates. Anyway, I'd better get back to school. I'll get Braden to give you a call once this barbeque is organised.'

'Thanks, Callie, you're a good friend.'

Harry glanced at his watch; Laura should be home by now. He might go home and have lunch with her. It was so quiet here. He knew he'd been a little bit distant lately, but the decision he had to make was a big one, and he wanted to give it lots of thought; he didn't want to pressure her into anything that she didn't want to do.

He decided to walk home to get a bit of exercise and was pleased as he turned into their street and saw Laura's car in the driveway.

He tapped lightly on the door before he pushed it open. 'Laura, it's only me. I've come home for lunch.'

All was quiet. He walked through the house, but there was no sign of her, apart from some parcels on the kitchen table, and it didn't look like any of them would hold a very big vase.

He walked through the laundry and closed his eyes at the familiar smell. The old-fashioned laundry had a concrete floor and a concrete tub that reminded him of his childhood when they had a similar set-up in Maryborough. The same damp concrete smell brought back some nostalgic feelings. He missed his family; his parents had long passed away, and he had been an only child. Over the past few years, his aunt and uncles had all gone as well. Now, he was pretty much the only Higgins left.

He went down the three steps that led to the back door and pushed it open. There she was, sitting on the back porch.

Laura jumped and put a hand to her chest. 'Oh, Harry, you gave me a fright.'

'I came home to have lunch with you. What are you doing out here?'

Laura's eyes were full of tears, and he hurried over and sat beside her, picking up both of her hands and holding them tightly.

'Sweetheart, what's wrong? Are you all right? You're not sick, are you? Nothing's happened, has it? Did you get some bad news from New Zealand?'

'I'm fine; it's just a few things I want to talk to you about. But first of all, I want to ask you one thing.' Her eyes were wide as she held his.

'Ask away, sweetheart.'

Her eyes brightened at the endearment, and she squeezed his hands back. 'Just one question, Harry. I just want to ask you one thing.'

He was quiet as he looked at her, and her eyes held his as she asked, 'Do you still love me?' Tears hovered on her lower lashes.

Harry's eyes widened and distress crossed his face. 'Sweetheart, I'm so sorry I've been preoccupied lately, and I feel terrible you have to ask that. The answer is a simple yes. Of course, I love you; I couldn't imagine life without you, Laura. I adore you; you've pre-empted me. There's something I've been working up to asking you, but I've been giving it a lot of thought first. That's why I've been quiet. I didn't want to pressure you.'

'I thought you were wanting to break up with me,' she said. 'You've been so quiet.'

'Love, I'm so sorry. Come here.' Harry stood and lifted Laura to her feet, and then he sat down and gestured for her to sit on his knee.

He wrapped his arms around her waist and rested his cheek against hers.

'Laura Adnum, you have no idea how much I love you. I thought love had gone forever for me when Jenny died, but then I met you. I was going to take you away and find a beautiful place. I was going to ask you to marry me.'

She drew a short breath, and her eyes widened. 'You . . . you want to marry me?'

'Of course I want to marry you. With all my heart. Laura, my dear love, will you do me the honour of becoming Mrs Higgins?'

Laura's arms went around his neck as he

held her. 'Harry . . . oh, Harry, I love you so much. Of course, I'll marry you, but you might not want to marry me when I tell you my news.'

'Why? What's wrong? Why were you sitting out here crying?'

As he watched her, her lower lip trembled. 'Come on, sweetheart. Tell me what's wrong.'

'Harry? I'm pregnant; you're going to be a dad.'

CHAPTER 14

The three boys ran ahead as Callie and Braden put the twins into the double stroller When Braden had called into the shed earlier in the week to invite them out to the station the new owners had asked if he would mind having a function at the shed on Saturday night instead of coming out to *Kilcoy Station*.

'But we'd love to come out there soon,' Greg had assured him.

'Not a problem at all, mate,' he replied. 'This way, you can get to know more of the townsfolk in one go.'

'We've had a lot of people calling in. There's been interest in the place and lots of questions. So, we figured that if we have everyone here on Saturday night, we can get the usual pub crowd and have a bit of a talk about what we're doing in town.'

'Sounds good to me,' Braden had said.

Callie and Braden were surprised to see how many cars had pulled up on the road between the park and the two new buildings. Most of the townspeople would've walked there tonight, so it appeared there was a lot of interest from people living on outlying properties. Craig Wilson and Quinn Calthorpe had told him they wouldn't miss it. Jon and Fallon were coming, and Ruth said she was keen to see it too.

Sophie and Kent were already here; he'd noticed their car parked at the end of the road near the church. Harry and Laura had said that they'd be here too. Braden bumped into them at the supermarket, and from their purchases, It was apparent they were having some sort of celebratory meal.

'That's good because Laura looked a bit off the other day, and Harry looked tired when I saw him at the hospital. Whatever was bothering him, he must've got it sorted,' Callie said when he told her that he'd seen them.

'I'm sure we'll find out if there's any news,' Braden said.

'What sort of news do you mean?' Callie asked with a frown. 'They're not moving away, are they?'

Braden tried to look innocent and shrugged. He hadn't told Callie he'd noticed the ring on Laura's finger. It was up to Laura and Harry to share their news, and there was a chance he might have misunderstood. It could be a ring from her previous marriage.

Callie drew a sharp breath as they pushed the pram around the back of the first building and looked up at Braden. Her eyes were wide.

'It's pretty incredible, isn't it?' he said.

'How can somebody do something with the previously dry grass, and now it looks like a fairy garden?' she said.

149

Braden looked around. 'They must have used some damn good fertiliser when they put the turf down.'

He knew they'd had landscapers up from Charleville, and they'd done a mighty fine job of getting a beautiful lawn from the back of the big paved area that came off the edge of the shed. There were dozens of tables with wine glasses and tea lights and fairy lights hanging above them from the pergola that somehow already had standard roses growing through the slats.

It looked like a wedding venue, and from all accounts, the group were planning on having functions like that at the back of the shed.

Sophie and Kent were standing at the edge of the lawn, Kent nursing Ruby as they chatted with Emily and Luke.

Sophie's eyes were wide, and she was saying, 'You pair, I do not believe it.'

Jenna and Josh walked over and joined them as Braden and Callie approached.

'I know,' Jenna said. 'I was lucky enough to be—well you could call me the bridesmaid but I suppose I was the witness.'

Callie looked curiously at Emily, and Emily held up her left hand, and then Luke held up his too. Shiny gold wedding rings were on their ring fingers.

'Go on, get out of it. Don't tell me you two snuck off and got married?'

'Yes, we did. Last Saturday. We couldn't wait for the pub to reopen to have our reception, so we decided we wanted to get married straight away.'

'Congratulations!' There were hugs and kisses all around as people came up and congratulated Luke and Emily. Ophelia put her cheek up, insisting on a kiss each time someone kissed Emily's cheek. 'Kiss me, kiss me too,' she said.

'Anyway,' Emily looked up at Luke, 'Tell them what you've just decided and organised, love.'

'We are going to be the first wedding function here at "The Shed" in a couple of weeks,' he said.

'Greg was saying that they've got a liquor license, and they're refurbishing the pub, the downstairs bars, the restaurant and the bistro, and the upstairs rooms, and it's going to take a little bit longer than they thought, so they're going to get this one off the ground. It's sort of going to be like a semi-pub with drinks every afternoon, and they've got Sean over from the pub to cook meals in the shed until the pub is ready.'

'Cook, where can he cook?' Braden asked. 'Do they know how fussy Sean is?'

Sophie looked at Braden. 'Go in there, bro,

and have a look. There's a whole commercial kitchen in the back of that second shed. It's supposed to be storage for the stuff they're putting in the shop shed.' As she was speaking, Greg and Chloe walked over.

'Hi, everyone, welcome to "The Shed".'

Chloe looked up at her husband with a smile. 'Everyone in town had been referring to it as "the shed". We've decided that we're going to call our new department store and function venue, "The Shed". What do you think about that?'

Braden grinned. 'Works for me. Just what the town needs.'

'Anyway, guys, come and sit down, grab a drink. I hope you didn't bring anything because it's all on us tonight.'

Greg walked away and greeted the next group of people. Sophie leaned over to Braden. 'How can they afford all this? My goodness, they've bought at least six houses in town. Lex and Rosie, who I met earlier, have got a little property out on the river. They built these two sheds. They're refurbishing the pub, which they bought, and they've bought the butcher shop. That's all that we know about.'

'None of our business, Sophie. Maybe they've come into an inheritance or something. Anyway, they all seem like really good people, and I think it's great that they've come to town and given Augathella a big injection of enthusiasm and rebuilding.'

'Oh, I'm not criticising,' she said. 'I think it's wonderful. But look, they're feeding a third of the district tonight, and Sean is in there in his absolute element.'

'Let's just enjoy ourselves.' Braden hugged his sister. 'Anyway, sis, you're looking well. Getting a bit more sleep than we are, I guess.'

'She's a little beauty, just like her mum.

Very well-behaved, very serene, very quiet.'

Braden laughed so loudly that Callie turned around. 'What are you two fighting about now?'

It was a wonderful evening with two stand-out moments.

The first one was when Greg and the rest of the group who had come to town stood up and told the townsfolk what their plans were. After outlining everything they were doing, there was a huge round of applause, and Braden was pleased to see how happy they all looked.

The second highlight of the night was the one that he had suspected, and he kept his face bland. When Dr Harry had taken the microphone after Greg finished speaking and announced that Laura had agreed to marry him.

Again, there was a standing ovation. Dr Harry had come to town a year ago and met Braden's sister-in-law, and they had fallen in love.

'Soph, can you keep an eye on the twins for us?' Braden tugged at Callie's hand. 'Come on, we're going to be the first to congratulate them.'

He walked over and held out his arms to Laura. 'Congratulations, sis. I'm pleased. You couldn't have picked a nicer guy.' He turned around and shook Harry's hand. 'You look after my sister-in-law, won't you, Dr Harry?'

'I certainly will.'

The night was full of joy, as the children ran around the paddocks until well after dark.

Braden smiled at Callie as the three boys, and the twins all fell asleep as soon as the car started.

CHAPTER 15

The wedding

Braden had been chuffed when Laura had asked him to give her away at the wedding. And Callie blinked back tears when Laura had asked her to be her bridesmaid along with Jenny Riley.

Jenny had harrumphed a few times. 'I'm too old to be a bridesmaid.'

'Well, you're my matron of honour if you don't want to be bridesmaid,' Laura said. 'I'm so grateful for your friendship over the past few months, Jenny.'

Emily and Luke's wedding breakfast at "The Shed" had been a huge success the weekend following the welcome dinner. The pub was open again and doing a roaring trade.

Now on this last weekend in March, Laura,

Callie, and Jenny were at the Higgins house getting ready to go to "The Shed" for the ceremony and reception.

Harry had stayed overnight at the Riley's house with Tom, who was his best man.

'I'm so sorry that Ben and Amelia have gone away,' Jenny said as they were waiting to be picked up by Kent in a vintage car loaned by Craig Wilson's father. They would've so enjoyed these last few weeks in town.' Amelia and Ben had taken the baby up to the Foley property in the Gulf country to spend some time with her parents

'Oh my God, Laura, you look absolutely beautiful,' Jenny said.

Laura's dress was off the shoulder with lace cap sleeves. The dress was slim-fitting and had a short train sweeping from the back.

'You're glowing.' Callie held her breath as Laura put her hand on her flat stomach and smiled.

A secret smile.

'There's a reason for that,' she said, 'but we're not making it public yet.'

'Oh Laura, you're having a baby!' Jenny said.

Laura nodded. 'We are, but it's just between the three of us for the time being. We're waiting to tell everyone until I get to the three-month mark.'

'Here's the car now,' Callie said as she heard a car door close in the driveway. Her heart filled with love as Braden came to the door looking handsome in his good suit.

'Ready, Laura?' he asked.

'I am. More than ready.' Laura was cool and calm as she took the hand that Braden held out to her.

It only took a few minutes to drive to "The Shed".

Callie was taken aback by the number of locals standing on the side of the footpath as the vintage car made its way slowly down the streets. Cheers and waves came from all ages, from school children to the folk from the aged-care facility; Harry and Laura were well-loved by the community, even after only a year in town. And once again Callie's heart filled as she felt proud to be a member of this community.

Tears pricked her eyes as she spotted Rory, Nigel, and Petie standing on the footpath near the park in the suits they'd hired for them in Charleville.

They all looked so grown up, and Rory was the image of Braden. She grinned as she noticed Nigel, pulling at the neck of his shirt.

Dear Nigel, he was their character, that's for sure.

Braden helped Laura from the front of the

car and waited while Jenny and Callie climbed out of the back seat. They were both dressed in matching soft peach dresses.

The boys walked ahead, and soon the strands of the Wedding March drifted from inside the building.

Laura was serene as Braden waited with her beside the flower-decked arch at the door. Nigel and Rory followed Petie and led Jenny and Callie down the aisle to the front of the room where the celebrant waited with Harry and Tom Riley.

The music swelled and Callie's eyes filled with tears as Braden escorted his sister-in-law down the aisle and Harry took her hand, love shining from his face.

***

Rosie stood with Chloe at the edge of the lawn. 'We've done good,' she said softly

'Yes, it was a lovely wedding,' Chloe said.

They watched as Harry swept Laura around the dance floor.

Rosie shook her head. 'Yes, the wedding was lovely, but I mean we've made a good choice. I think we're all going to be very happy in this town.'

'We are. Very happy. We'll raise our families here, and we'll leave part of ourselves in this town when we move on,' Chloe said. Her eyes held that faraway look. 'Augathella is a very special place,' she said softly.

An Augathella Easter

Available in print on Amazon and Annie's store

May 2024

https://annieseatonstore.ecwid.com/An-Augathella-Easter-Pre-order-May-2024-p630576883

Amazon:

https://www.amazon.com.au/gp/product/B0CW31XGWW

OTHER PRINT BOOKS from ANNIE

Available on Annie's store and Amazon:

https://annieseatonstore.ecwid.com/

New Series: The Daughters of The Darling

1: From Across the Sea (April 2024)

2. Over the River (September 2024)

Other books

Whitsunday Dawn

Undara

Osprey Reef

East of Alice

Porter Sisters Series

Kakadu Sunset

Daintree

Diamond Sky

Hidden Valley

Larapinta

Kakadu Dawn

Pentecost Island Series

Pippa

Eliza

Nell

Tamsin

Evie

Cherry

Odessa

Sienna

Tess

Isla

Also available in three boxed sets

Books 1-3

Books 4-6

Books 7-10

The Augathella Girls Series

Outback Roads

Outback Sky

Outback Escape

Outback Wind

Outback Dawn

Outback Moonlight

Outback Dust

Outback Hope

Sunshine Coast Series

Waiting for Ana

The Trouble with Jack

Healing His Heart

Sunshine Coast Boxed Set

The Richards Brothers Series

The Trouble with Paradise

Marry in Haste

Outback Sunrise

Richards Brothers Boxed Set

Bondi Beach Love Series

Beach House

Beach Music

Beach Walk

Beach Dreams

The House on the Hill

Second Chance Bay Series

Her Outback Playboy

Her Outback Protector

Her Outback Haven

Her Outback Paradise

The McDougalls of Second Chance Bay Boxed Set

Love Across Time Series

Come Back to Me

Follow Me

Finding Home

The Threads that Bind

Love Across Time 1-4 Boxed Set

Bindarra Creek

Worth the Wait

Full Circle

Secrets of River Cottage

A Clever Christmas

A Bindarra Creek Duo

A Place to Belong

Four Seasons Short and Sweet

Ten Days in Paradise

Follow the Sun

Others

Deadly Secrets

Adventures in Time

Silver Valley Witch

The Emerald Necklace

Christmas with the Boss

Her Christmas Star

An Aussie Christmas Duo (the two Christmas novellas)

ABOUT THE AUTHOR

Annie lives in Australia, on the beautiful north coast of New South Wales. She sits in her writing chair and looks out over the tranquil Pacific Ocean.

She writes contemporary romance and loves telling stories that always have a happily ever after. She lives with her very own hero of many years and they share their home with Toby, the naughtiest dog in the universe, and Barney, the ragdoll puss, who hides when the four grandchildren come to visit.

Stay up to date with her latest releases at her website: http://www.annieseaton.net

AWARDS

2023: Winner of the long contemporary RUBY award for Larapinta

Finalist for the NZ KORU Award 2018 and 2020.

Winner ...Best Established Author of the Year 2017 AUSROM

Longlisted for the Sisters in Crime Davitt Awards 2016, 2017, 2018, 2019

Finalist in Book of the Year, Long Romance, RWA Ruby Awards 2016 Kakadu Sunset

Winner ...Best Established Author of the Year 2015 AUSROM

Winner ...Author of the Year 2014 AUSROM

Best Established Author, Ausrom Readers' Choice 2017 Book of the Year

Milton Keynes UK
Ingram Content Group UK Ltd.
UKHW010635040324
438885UK00001B/41